Praise for *Esquire Ball:*
Stories from the Great Black Swamp

Lisa Slage Robinson has a great gift for making readers
care about her characters; we want what they want;
we dread what they dread. And she is an expert in bad
behaviour. Many of her women are not as nice as they
seem. *Esquire Ball* is a dazzling and irresistible collection.

—Margot Livesey, author of *The Road from Belhaven*

In *Esquire Ball,* Lisa Slage Robinson spins a set of stories
that are not just linked but entangled: a sister blessed and
saddled with a darling brother dumped on her doorstep by
her absentee father; a lawyer who finds himself trying to
con his colleagues to aide an ailing widow and her unofficial
granddaughter; a young man on the verge of professional
success who takes to the swamps to replace the fiancée who
abandoned him. Though many of the stories take place in
courtrooms and law offices, these are characters who are at
heart lawless, irrepressible, who resist the world's efforts and
even their own desperate desires to become respectable and
instead lead the reader through twisted, intriguing paths.

—Anjali Sachdeva, author of *All the Names they Used for God*

Esquire Ball

Stories from the Great Black Swamp

LISA SLAGE ROBINSON

Black Lawrence Press

Black Lawrence Press

Executive Editor: Diane Goettel
Book Cover Design: Zoe Norvell
Cover Art: "Frog" by Kateryna Repa
Book Interior Design: Serena Solin

ISBN: 9781625571809

Published 2026 by Black Lawrence Press.
Printed in the United States.

Table of Contents

For my daughters,
Caroline and Kendall

My salad days,
When I was green in judgment: cold in blood.

Antony and Cleopatra, Shakespeare

DON'T CALL ME A THIEF. I am a collector. I would never pocket, for example, something so pedestrian as Wallenda's gold cigarette lighter or one of Mad Dog's monogramed cufflinks. It is the ineffable I seek. Like that time, when one of the partners at my law firm asked me to babysit, I reached under his sleeping nine-year-old's pillow and snatched the kid's pointy canine. I soaked the macaroni-encrusted and blood-stained tooth in hydrogen peroxide for two days before I tucked it into a robin's nest, the one I pinched from the underbelly of my neighbor's downspout. The curiosity now sits on my office credenza, next to my stapler and rolodex.

I discovered my need for tokens when I left home with my high heels, casebooks, and law school diploma, eager to forget the people who had broken me in one way or the other, but not quite willing to give up the sting. From Mom, I took the delicate China teacup and saucer with the hand-painted forget-me-nots. From Margot, her liquid eyeliner of course. From Jimmer, a lock of his curly brown hair that I snipped after he passed out on our yellow chintz sofa. From Mrs. Stevens, a solitary opera glove with real pearl buttons. From my father, there wasn't much to choose from. Other than a generous supply of unpaid bills, he hadn't left much behind. I considered the blue dolphin ashtray, his frequent flyer's plaque, the broken string of rosary beads, and his scratched Sears Craftsman with the steepled lid, a rattle of nails, a claw hammer and screwdrivers inside. I settled on the toolbox hoping that it would come in handy someday.

Now, a year later, standing outside Victor Sinclair's house, toolbox in hand, I wonder what I will find. If there's anything worth spiriting away.

Victor Sinclair doesn't know me, the associate assigned to his case, but I know him with an intimacy earned from months of the purgatory known as document review, sorting through boxes of musty papers, edges gnawed by invisible creatures, purchase orders, promissory notes scribbled on napkins, interoffice memos, scores of schematics, blueprints, and quarterly reports.

In all my wildest black-and-white Perry Mason fantasies, I never envisioned myself dungeoned in crawl spaces and damp warehouse basements, searching for something relevant. Where was the courtroom? The polished mahogany banisters? The interrogation? The smoking gun? I found instead, mingled with Victor Sinclair's business records, a crumpled stash of domestic clutter: cancelled checks for the dog groomer, the housekeeper, the handyman. A grocery shopping list that included sardines, sugar, and grenadine. Restaurant receipts. Christmas cards. A ribbon of photo booth pictures of a younger Victor Sinclair and his wife, all kissy face and laughing. Polaroids of the kids he never sees, Denny and Nicole, hamming it up in puffy snowsuits and sandy swimsuits. Undelivered letters of apology. *Crime and Punishment*, *The Art of the Deal*, a dog-eared copy of Sun Tzu's *The Art of War*. A divorce decree.

I started copying his signature. I obsessed over the spiked cadence of his letters, the way they slanted forcefully to the right, the deeply engraved impressions his pen left in its wake, *Victor Sinclair*, the heartbeat of something I couldn't articulate, something mysterious, something obscene. I read his books. I memorized his phone number, social security number, his birthday. To entertain myself, I pieced together a life; the missing details, I made up.

The circular scar on his upper left arm from his smallpox vaccine. His first hernia exam, when the school nurse deftly cradled his balls and asked him to cough, his erection and the harsh rebuke from the nurse's ruler. His first girlfriend named Marguerite or Daisy or Rose, tiny and delicate, yet athletic, a dancer or a gymnast, the smartest girl he knew. The wrestling trophies, the toes he lost mountain climbing. Of his adulthood, I am less certain. But I recognize that charming billboard smile, the catastrophes that lie in wait.

Yeah, I know Victor Sinclair like a tattered paperback. He's an earworm, like last summer's party song.

Dad's toolbox feels heavy. My wrist aches from the weight of it. A bruise blossoms where it banged against my thigh during the walk from my car, past sagging Victorians, to Victor Sinclair's dilapidated arts and crafts bungalow, a place where unfaithful husbands and lousy fathers go. In the distance, far, far off, a basketball dribbles then bounces off a backboard again and again and again. My ears yearn for an occasional swoosh, a clatter of bikes thrown as their riders hop off, a jump rope skipping, peals of laughter. Here, such sounds don't exist.

I circle around to the back of the house, push past bramble bushes, sidestep the carcass of an old hot water heater and squish, ankle deep, through a pile of grass clippings and rotting compost muck. The lattice that skirts the back porch is busted; critter-sized holes blink. I don't stop to worry about what may be lurking underneath.

The back door is old and it doesn't take much imagination or many tools from Dad's toolbox to jimmy the lock. With an Allen wrench and a putty knife, the tumblers click, the knob turns, the door swings open, and I'm in.

The ants are the first thing I notice. Then a sink full of dishes, then the smell of burnt frying pan and I'm confused because Victor Sinclair is supposed to be out of town. Later, I will wonder why I didn't flee. But when you wallow in the extremes of love and hate, you can't see, refuse to see, the warning signs. There's just you and your obsession.

Victor Sinclair had been my constant companion for twelve months, the half-n-half in my coffee, the brown sugar in my instant oatmeal, the run in my stocking, the stitch in my side during a long run. And now the case is over, leaving me empty and confused.

My daydreams conjured a dashing, complicated man, a tragic figure brooding over his diminishing wealth. Even now, I picture him in a crisp white shirt—the kind with billowing sleeves, a burgundy cravat, a velvet waistcoat, and tall boots polished to an immaculate shine, like the man in a gothic romance novel, a man's man with a valet. But there's no wife hidden in the attic; she's presiding over the family mansion on the other side of town while he's relegated to this house of shame, the brittle bones of his empire. What am I supposed to do with all that?

The ants on Victor Sinclair's floor, hundreds of specks swarming a solitary crumb, slay me. I know now that it's Victor Sinclair's redemption I came to retrieve, and I will not find it in this dreary little kitchen that doesn't even have a table and chairs. I want to weep. Instead, I kick off my shoes, throw them at Dad's toolbox waiting on the porch. I slam the door.

Under the sink I find rubber gloves and rags. On my hands and knees, I scrub the floor, erase the convention of ants and my own footprints, the clumps of grass and backyard muck I tracked in. I wash the dishes, place them on the drain board, scour the sink and toss the dirty towels and my soiled jeans and socks into the stackable Kenmore, grateful for its odd presence in the kitchen closet where normally a mop and broom and dustpan would be. For good measure, I toss in my T-shirt as well. And then I'm just in my black bra and matching panties like I own the place.

In the fridge I find brown mustard and pickles, four sticks of butter, a carton of orange juice and a loaf of bread and a bottle of Beefeaters. I unscrew the cap, take a swig. It dribbles past my lips and onto my chin, which I wipe with the back of my hand. The cupboard doors are warped and it takes three hard tugs to reveal the contents inside: a box of Triscuits, two cans of sardines, a single place setting of buttery yellow dishes, and three vintage jelly jars. I grab the one with Sylvester and Tweety Bird, pour myself a glass. Now that it has warmed up a bit, the gin is vibrant, foresty. It echoes Christmas trees and sleigh rides and stolen kisses and burns all the way down. Perhaps I'll take Sylvester and Tweety Bird. But, for now, I leave them on the counter.

Beyond the kitchen, there's only the living room. An old brown carpet has been taken up, rolled into a log. Two bean bag chairs flank an old TV set with rabbit ears. Someone has been removing wallpaper. I pick at the edges until my fingernails take hold, then peel a satisfying swath of yellow chrysanthemum and vining foliage from the wall. I move through the room escorted by ghosts. The steps creak as I climb to the second floor.

The bathroom at the top of the stairs hosts a cast iron tub. I imagine it filled with almost scalding water and suds spilling over the sides, dipping first one toe and then the other, easing myself in. I imagine the privilege of waiting for someone to come home. The last time I had been in a tub like this was at my grandmother's just after Margot disappeared and Dad left again. My grandmother scolded me for crying because once I started there seemed to be no way to make it stop. With a washcloth and a bar of soap she scrubbed my skin raw and told me that no one had a right to be happy in this life. That crying was a chore best done in private. Or not at all.

I wander into Victor Sinclair's bedroom. Like the rest of the house, the furnishings are spare, a queen size bed with no headboard, rust-colored sheets and duvet tousled from a recent sleep, a wooden side chair, a mirror. My fingers trail the top of the dresser. I sniff Victor Sinclair's cologne, a smoky mix of pine needles, moss, and spice, like disco in the swamp. With my index finger, I sort the pile of pocket change into quarters, nickels, pennies, and dimes. I examine Victor Sinclair's hairbrush, pull out a few strands of hair, watch them float to the ground, one by one. Try on his hat, a grey felt fedora the kind that grandpas and gangsters wear.

From his closet, I pull out a suitcoat, banker's gray to match the fedora. Victor Sinclair's a big man. The sleeves fall past my wrists, the coat covers my knees. I pose for the mirror, tilt the hat to a jaunty angle, turn from side to side, thinking the hat would look so much better if I still had my long hair. I pull out wisps of dark curls, to better frame my face. See myself in the reflection as others must see me, shortish with sharp features, pointy nose, squinty eyes, one punctuated with a half-moon scar, a too-large grin, muscular thighs. Wide hips that don't match the rest of my frame. Too much and too little. I tug at a long curl so that it covers the scar; it gives me a secret agent look. I wonder what it feels like to be Victor Sinclair or my dad or any man who has everything and loses it all, yet never accepts responsibility, never accepts defeat. Not even a phoenix rising from the ashes because they don't acknowledge the ashes exist.

I'm startled by a loud clearing of a throat. A bemused reprimand. My heart thumps and I can feel heat creeping up my spine and rouging my face. A young man leans against the door frame, smirking like he's Cool Hand Luke. Shirtless, a gold chain sits above his boney sunburned clavicle. At least six feet tall, broad-shouldered and so skinny that surely his bones ache from the architecture of him. A six pack of beer is tucked under one long arm, another he dangles by the yoke of its plastic netting. There's no mistaking who he is. He looks exactly like his father. He doesn't seem alarmed or surprised to see me.

"You must be my father's new girlfriend," Denny says. His voice deeper than I expect. Because of the photos, I always think of him as a little boy but I realize that he must be in college by now.

"Why would you say that?" I take off the hat, toss it on the bed, smooth back my hair.

"There's always a new one," he says, "after he ditches the last one." The cans of beer clink as he sets them down on the dresser.

"How do you know I'm not the cleaning lady?" I say, rolling up the sleeves of the suit jacket.

He pulls a blue and silver can from its plastic tether. Wipes the top on his white painter's pants. He appraises the ribbon of skin and swatches of lace not covered by his father's coat.

"You're not as pretty as the last one." He pulls the tab. Click. Thwup. Takes a swig.

"Are you having a party?" I cross my arms over my chest.

"Nope. Just came back to get wasted." He chugs the beer like he's just returned from the desert. Like he's dying from thirst. He crunches the can, tosses it, a perfect arc into the wastepaper basket. Grabs another. Pops the lid.

"Well listen. I'm just going to get my jeans." I shuffle in the direction of the door, my escape hatch, to the downstairs and the brilliant stackable Kenmore, the back door, my shoes, my toolbox. He shifts his column of bones from right then left as I try to step around him.

"Size six? Not ready yet. I already checked. The last girl? Debbie? She was, is, a size two."

"I'm just going to check anyway." I try again and again to get around him but he's too quick. He blocks me with fakes and shuffle steps as if we're playing basketball.

He laughs. "Wanna dance?"

"Not really. Running is more my thing."

He pulls yet another can, offers it to me.

"No thank you."

"I insist," he says shoving it into my hands.

I take it, like it's nothing at all. Me, an uninvited guest, nearly naked under Victor Sinclair's suit. What was that quote? From Sun Tzu? *The supreme art of war is to subdue the enemy without fighting.*

"It's not that you're not pretty. It's just that Dad usually goes for…" He pauses to summon the right words. "Chicks that are hot."

"Assuming I care, that's supposed to make me feel better?"

"Ah shit. You know," he says waiving his beer in the air. "They wear lots of makeup and jewelry and high heels with their jeans. And when they have a sleepover—they don't play dress up—they usually prance around in some silky negligee. You look more like the type of girl who'd date a guy like me."

"What type of girl is that?" I say.

"Someone my age for starters," he says. "And nice." I can't help smiling. Being pegged as nice doesn't sound like an insult coming from him. He's mistaken of course, but for a moment I wish it were true. "My name is Denny by the way. Denny Becker." He shifts his can from right to left, I do the same, take his outstretched hand, note the firm grip, the paint-speckled knuckles, the callouses on his fingertips. "It used to be Sinclair but that was some stupid ass name Dad made up. Said it sounded like success. You know what really sounds like success? Denny and Debbie."

"Size two Debbie?'

"Yeah." He lifts his chin.

"Dad invited me and my older sister to his cottage on Kelly's Island. Said we could bring a friend. I didn't need one because my sister invited Debbie. I had it all figured out. I had this enormous crush on her, you know? She always joked with me and put her arm around me. Told me her secrets. She had these cut-off jean shorts. I just always thought she'd be my first."

I open my beer. Take an empathetic sip.

"You know where my father is now?" I do know, but I shake my head. "He's sitting in a sweat lodge cleansing his spirit, smoking out his demons." He grabs the discarded hat by the pinch, places it first on his head, then settles it back on mine. "You know where Debbie is today? With my sister at the clinic. Getting rid of his other demon." Something I didn't know.

He clinks his can into mine. Chugs. Squashes it. Tosses it into the basket.

"I'm hungry. You hungry?" He takes my hand, laces his fingers with mine. I let him, like I'm nineteen or twenty, like I'm foolish and innocent, open to the serendipity of the moment. Together we creak down the stairs, back to the sad little kitchen.

"You didn't need to clean this crappy place. I'd have gotten to it eventually. Just been a little busy lately. I swim laps every morning at six to keep my scholarship. Then I lifeguard at the country club. On my days off, I paint houses and work on this shithole. Have to build back my college fund that somehow magically disappeared. Disappearing funds, it's a trend in my family. My dad's a real Houdini with money. Perhaps you read about it in the paper?"

Denny opens the cupboard with a swift tug. Grabs a can of sardines and the box of crackers, hands them to me. "You mind if we retire to the drawing room? I've been stripping wallpaper and spackling holes all day."

I wonder if he's found any crazy ladies trapped in the wallpaper. If he's released them from their prison. If it's their needy presence I feel in the house, urging me on.

"Sure," I say, following him and the intoxicating scent of boy— sweat mingled with chlorine and sunshine and soap. "I've been admiring your handywork. Looks like fun."

"Shit," he says. He shakes his head. His scaffolding collapses into the bean bag chair. He tugs the hem of his father's coat, urging me to sit down beside him. His back curves like a C. He breathes from his concave belly; I watch it go in and out. His skin is taut, stretched against every knob of every bone. I imagine my hand trailing the pickets of his ribcage. I wonder how it might feel, his sharp angles pressed against my soft curves. What it would feel like to be his first, to teach him, this wounded son, the pleasures of the flesh. I lean in for a kiss. He pulls away.

"Don't take this the wrong way. I'd really like to kiss you," he says, "but then I'd be just like my dad."

"I told you, Denny. I'm *not* your father's girlfriend."

"Who are you, then?"

"Don't worry about it." I whisper, my mouth so close I can almost taste his lips. "I'm nobody. I'm just a thief."

MR. CAMPBELL IMAGINED HER BROKEN-HOME SWAGGER, the fringe of her cut-off jean shorts, the sweet curve of her jailbait ass. And those long, lean legs climbing the ladder, rung after rung, four stories high. Ellie laughing at that chicken shit Tom before disappearing into the belly of silo #9. How she might have sung that annoying country song she always belted—just to hear her own voice echo, a husky alto graveling against steel. He imagined the confident stomp of her borrowed work boots, a size too big, breaking up clumps of moist grain, kicking the sides of the mammoth vessel, dislodging kernels, moldy and green. Beads of sweat collecting at the nape of her neck, underneath her ponytail. Perhaps she stopped to pull the ends of her T-shirt up to wipe her mouth, up to cover her nose, to mask that foul fermented odor, what he knew smelled like rotten potatoes, like cemetery dirt.

In the bin, Ellie had neither harness nor rope, nothing tethering her to safety. Even if the company had provided one, he was pretty sure she wouldn't have used it.

He remembered the night he drove her home from band camp hours after her mother had failed to show. He couldn't stop looking at her lips, bruised rosebuds, swollen and tender from playing the flugel-horn. How he had wanted, desperately, to kiss her but asked, instead, what she planned to do for the rest of the summer. She shrugged her shoulders. The lifeguard position over at the Y hadn't panned out once they discovered she never learned to swim. She supposed she'd study for the SATs from an outdated book she borrowed from the library. She wanted to be a lawyer, someday, even though everyone told her she'd never make it. *What about you, Mr. Campbell?* She lingered on the word "mister," tugged on it like tufts of cotton candy melting in her mouth. *Since you're such a good student teacher, maybe you could show me how to float?*

Instead of dropping her off at the section 8 housing complex over by Southwyck Mall, he took her to the quarry. It was getting dark and before he had time to unlace his shoes, she'd already stripped down to her underwear, a disappointing functional ensemble, whitish-gray and tattered. Without hesitating, without pausing to read the caution sign, she jumped off the rocks, plunging into the icy cold water, twenty-two feet deep. She refused to apologize after he dove in, fully clothed, to save her. He dragged her, as she sputtered and coughed, back to the rocks. *I thought it would be like in the movies, you know, where the dad throws the baby into the middle of the pool, and the kid just starts swimming like a tadpole. You should have given me a few more minutes, Mr. Campbell.*

Ellie believed strongly in her instincts. And soon, he did too. When it was she who kissed him that night, shivering in their wet clothes amongst the cattails and croaking frogs, then later in her lemon yellow bedroom underneath her glow-in-the dark stars. The way she moved her hips, the way she clutched his shoulders, pulling him closer when he said he should stop. In the quiet moments afterward, as he marveled at her soft unblemished face, she told him things. How she was left alone to tend to herself most days and nights, her father gone and her mother always working. How her mother, afraid of everything, wore her fears like a black fur coat, an oppressive luxury she wrapped tight around both of them even in the heat. How her mother's fears had grafted onto Ellie's psyche and how Ellie had a coat too but hers was more like bunny rather than bear, lighter, easier to live with, easier to shed. Ellie couldn't wait any longer to live and breathe.

When he wasn't taking college classes or teaching band kids how to march in straight lines that segued into elaborate figure eights, Mr. Campbell worked at the grain elevators his family owned with the co-op. He suggested that, instead of drowning, perhaps she'd like to join his grain team. They were always short of seasonal help. He figured she could do paperwork, keep track of invoices, bills of lading, that sort of thing.

But Ellie couldn't be contained in that little pickle jar of an office. She'd finish the day's work, efficiently, accurately without complaint, in half the time it usually took. Then she'd bolt, flugelhorn in hand, march about the farm like she owned the place, alternately singing and playing her horn. The guys didn't mind on account of those jean shorts and her Tanya Tucker twang.

They were unloading the corn into a truck headed for the Port of Toledo when the auger got stuck. The steady flow had dwindled to a trickle. Mr. Campbell yelled over to Tom, told him that this was his lucky day to finally grow some balls, that it was his turn to walk down the corn. The heavy rains from the previous year had made the grain wet and clumpy, it stuck to the sides of the bin and gummed up the works. Climbing inside and breaking up the jam was the only way to get things moving again. Ellie jogged past the dawdling Tom, eager to prove she could do more than just shuffle paper. *I'm on it, Mr. Campbell.* She flashed a big toothy smile. He didn't stop her. Somehow he was certain she knew what to do.

No one at the co-op ever thought too much about the parade of horribles waiting for the teenagers sent down into the belly of the beast, the highly combustible grain dust, the toxic gases, the machinery that could chew off limbs, the grain itself, its insatiable appetite. They disregarded the one-page missives and diagrams sent by the government and taped to the breakroom wall.

Mr. Campbell was pleased when the corn started to flow again, this time at a brisk pace, when he heard Tom screaming to shut down the conveyor. Tom had reached the summit of the bin, just before a swirling vortex opened up, pulling Ellie down, swallowed in seconds in a sea of corn. Tom would later recall the horror to a local public radio station: Ellie gasping for breath as the weight of so many bushels of corn compressed her rib cage, then throat, then mouth. When she was completely engulfed, her ponytail lingered for one defiant moment until it too was gone.

Rescuers from three counties, Lucas and Wood and Sandusky, arrived: fire fighters, EMTs, machinery operators, police. On the outside, they cut holes into the vessel, so the grain could weep out the sides. On the inside, tethered to ropes, they worked to shovel her out.

A preacher and a team of lawyers from Toledo milled around, got in the way then whisked Mr. Campbell to the office where Ellie had processed forms. They coaxed the details from Mr. Campbell who, in between his sobs, deftly puzzled the jagged pieces back together into a liability-proof tale. The preacher patted his shoulder, told him to pray. The lawyers patted his shoulder, assuring him that no one ever goes to jail for things like this. *Even with reckless disregard for a known hazardous condition, even if the situation results in the worst possible outcome, it's just a misdemeanor, son. And the fines? Those get negotiated down to next to nothing.*

As the hours ticked by, twelve to be exact, Mr. Campbell indulged in his own creative thinking, fashioning a fairytale better than praying to God, Ellie as a tadpole, swimming not drowning in all that corn, Ellie breathing through her tadpole gills, Ellie emerging from the grain bin transformed into swan or mermaid or whatever human-tadpoles turn into.

When the rescue team pulled Ellie out, Mr. Campbell didn't want to look, but knew her beautiful skin was mottled, pock-marked like a golf ball, her rosebud mouth, her ears, her lungs filled with corn dust and debris, legs crushed into a single pulpy fin.

Salad Days

I DON'T LOOK LIKE A LAWYER. Everybody says so. I know what they're really thinking: *What's a nice girl like you doing in a place like this?* But I'm not as nice as I seem or nearly as mean as I'd like to be. I guess that's why I spent so much of my first year as a lawyer sorting documents, coaching the firm's softball team, and hanging portraits of dead partners on the walls of Strathy, McMahon's boardroom.

Jimmer says the word I'm looking for is tough or assertive or maybe even aggressive. But Jimmer is wrong and I told him so. I know from experience that a lawyer's success is a byproduct of a deep-seated meanness. Meanness like exhaust-stained slush as dark and cold and ugly as Main Street on a bitter January afternoon. That's what prompts the lawyers I know to represent the Almighty Client, right or wrong, without regard for the truth.

Before that thing with Norma, before the whole rotten mess stunk so bad that I could no longer ignore it, I cultivated my own little garden of meanness, first planting the seeds of observation and then watering it daily with practice. Without it, I knew I would be a failure. I didn't have to look far for inspiration. At Strathy, McMahon, I was surrounded by every sort of viper, opportunist, and backyard bully. Take Wallenda, for example. I coveted, among other things, his use of the English language. He peppered his sentences with hells and goddamns, fuckyou and fuckme. I admired the well-placed cocksucker, sonofabitch, or motherfucker which never failed to heighten the tension and sense of urgency in a room. Thus, in the spirit of perfecting my professional skills, I spent hours in front of the mirror parroting my mentor's turn of phrase. I'd say, *God damn it, you cocksucker, who the fuck told you that you could go home before you finished the goddamn brief?* In deep and husky staccato eighth notes. Just like Wallenda.

I'd practice those words as I pinned on my silk bowtie and straightened my steel-gray wool suit, trying not to laugh at myself. Not even the authority of *Dallas*-sized shoulder pads could lower my girlish voice or change how silly my face looked. Nevertheless, I persevered.

A year in and I already had a pretty good start. Behind my back, the other first years started calling me the Ice Princess. Preston Wade, one of the summer associates, told me. Despite or perhaps because of this notorious appellation, Preston confessed his affection for me one evening as we were rummaging through the boxes of documents that filled the entire thirteenth floor of the Toledo Edison Building. I suspected that "cold bitch" was my true moniker, but Preston lived his old money and polite society like a modern-day Ashley Wilkes.

Normally, he would have been long gone for the day. Summer associates scored salaries higher than the first years, offices with windows and a view, and deceptively light hours. At five o'clock sharp, like children released for recess, they spilled out of Strathy, McMahon's brass and mahogany doors into the partners' summertime playgrounds: Detroit for a Tigers game or Sandusky for cigars and a spin on Hillcrest's fishing boat or Windsor to drink beer with DeLuca and leer at the topless French-Canadian girls at The Playhouse or Cleopatra's. Face time at these fieldtrips, how you held your liquor, or your stomach on the choppy Lake Erie waters, or how artfully you slid your dollars into a dancer's tiny little G-string—these were the skills that got you an offer at Strathy, McMahon.

Unfortunately for Preston, Wallenda didn't care about the distinction between associates and summer associates and the niceties of recruitment outings.

"What the fuck are you doing?" Wallenda said as Preston, with briefcase in hand, loped past the War Room at 4:59 PM. "Get the fuck in here. We need your help."

On the thirteenth floor, rows of reinforced steel shelves blocked the sunlight that otherwise reflected off the muddy waters of the Maumee River. Thousands of papers, catalogues, manuals, letters, and contracts had been plucked from basements and attics, warehouses and limestone mines. The place smelled dank and musty like an antique shop. Dust motes floated in the fluorescent light.

"They warned me about you," Preston said as he pulled down a box labeled Box 1020 -Nuclear Power Plant, torque switch manuals. "Said you were *cold as ice*. Like that Foreigner song. Told me what you did to the mailroom guy. Said a few other things but I can't repeat them."

I wanted to say, I don't give a fuck about what they say. But I hadn't perfected my casual use of profanity yet. So I just laughed. Besides, I couldn't hold his revelations against him. He was awfully cute. Self-conscious and self-important in his navy-blue suit, tailored to perfection, a crisp white cotton button-down noosed with a natty yellow tie. His face looked like a Dove soap commercial, blemish free and not even a five o'clock shadow to mar its loveliness. Just a smattering of barely visible freckles on his pedigreed nose.

And later, when he pressed his hips against mine, my back against the steel shelves and cardboard boxes, how could I resist the temptation to accept his proffered lips? I pushed him away for just a second, contemplating whether or not I wanted to kiss a man outfitted by his parents or grandparents or some other distant long-forgotten relative. Would he taste like money, like champagne and caviar? For the purpose of research, I decided to give him a try.

"Aren't you afraid you'll get freezer burn?" I said.

"Nah." He grinned and tugged at the lapels of my department store blazer, pulling me closer.

For a moment, he was brave. And for a moment, so was I. He tasted homespun, like butterscotch, like more than just a wicked moment. His hands cradled my face and then his thumb gently traced the scar under my left eye. I wanted to stay there, in that moment. That's when the lump formed at the back of my throat, and my eyes burned. I bit him. Sunk my teeth into his bottom lip until I tasted blood.

"Ouch!" said Preston pulling away. A pinprick of red pearled before he licked it off. "You crazy…" he said catching himself before he yelled the word *bitch*. "Why'd you do that?"

"God, you're such a fuckin' baby," I said. My delivery, perfection. Preston straightened his tie and cleared his throat. He wiped his mouth with the back of his hand.

"You really don't feel much of anything, do you?" Preston said. He stared down into the box of engineering notes and then concluded, "You know, not in any way that is appropriate."

"There's a vending machine on this floor. I'm going to get Ding Dongs," I said. "Want anything?"

"No," he said.

"Suit yourself," I said as I walked out the door. It's not that I didn't feel anything. It's just that I controlled my exposure. Just like the engineers over at the nuclear power plant with their pressure valves and torque switches, I scheduled the release of my emotions, those toxic byproducts of daily living. Otherwise, we'd have a nuclear disaster on our hands.

Jimmer would probably agree with Preston which annoyed me. Who needed a conscience when you had Jimmer back home in Akron, judging you, whispering from a distance his theories of life into your ear? Jimmer in his faded Bob Dylan concert tee, raggedy jeans, and moldable mop of brown curls.

The last time I went home, Jimmer said, "You're going to explode. You know that don't you? Where'd you get this idea that you can just take everything that happens, shove it into some metaphorical box, scotch tape the lid shut and throw the whole mess away?" His fingers had roostered his hair into a cox comb—the result of an all-nighter pondering Kierkegaard.

We were eating jam sandwiches, two pieces of white bread slathered with French's yellow mustard and jammed together, because that was the only thing in the house to eat. Jimmer took a bite of his. Mustard oozed out the sides and onto the heel of his palm and down his wrist. Jimmer licked the mustard off his hand and then worked his way around the square of his sandwich. "You think the box disappears right? But it doesn't. It follows you everywhere you go. There's no magical shithole to dump it in. The only way to get rid of it is to feel it."

Yeah right. This advice coming from the guy who, in a fit of manic rage, threw the Christmas tree off the balcony of Mom's townhouse. The sound of ornaments crashing onto to the blacktop driveway below startling the neighbors awake and bringing the police to the building for the third time that month. Well into spring, we were still finding splinters of glass and strands of silver tinsel.

"You should come to my tribal drumming therapy," Jimmer said as he opened the freezer door, rummaged inside, and produced two misshaped ice cream sandwiches, white wrappers covered in ice crystals. "Dude, we got dessert!"

"Where's Mom?" I said snatching my prize.

"In bed."

"How many days?"

"Too many to count."

I nodded, tearing off the wrapper and tossing it on top of the overflowing waste basket.

"Dad?"

"Oh, well. You know, the usual," he said. Which meant Dad was off somewhere with wacky Darlene, her healing crystals and her homegrown weed. At least she kept him away from his Jack Daniels and the pills.

"Bills?"

"On the counter."

I licked the sides of the ice cream the way Jimmer licked his jam sandwich. Stale crystals stuck to my tongue. It tasted like a friendless summer vacation, the smack of my father's hand. Like broken bones.

I waited until the next day to lift the lid, to let it all out. After I pressed a few twenties into Jimmer's mustard-stained palms. After I sat on the end of Mom's bed, told her a handful of lies about how well the job was going. After I dusted off the pictures of Margot who would have turned thirty in the spring. After I grabbed the stack of bills, packed up the car and headed towards Toledo. I sobbed big ugly tears all the way to the Anthony Wayne Trail and well into Monday morning.

Then I showered, brushed my teeth, suited up, outlined my mouth with Bonnie Belle lip gloss, and shouted "fuck you" to the mirror as I put my smile back on my face.

I wondered if Wallenda stole away to some secret place to cry. If he mourned for the people he humiliated during depositions, people he buried in paperwork. Mourned for all those people who lost their jobs, their houses, their lives. The Great Wallenda, famous for death defying feats, nimbly traversing that tightrope between the spirit and the letter of the law. He practiced without a safety net. I wondered what would happen if he ever fell. Would he be buoyed by a grudging respect from all those people he bullied?

I felt protective of him. I rationalized that he couldn't help losing it every now and then. It frustrated him that everyone else's brain functioned so much slower than his. He'd sit in his leather chair—a boyish cowlick sprouting from his poker-straight, golden brown hair, some of which was always falling into his eyes. The ends had a slick, slightly greasy sheen from being brushed back with his fingers. His other hand preoccupied with an endless trail of cigarettes, shaking during the journey from the ashtray to his mouth. He tapped his pen and bounced his knee in pensive contemplation. His body in constant motion. I imagined his brain, too, with ideas jumping and bouncing and exploding. Sort of like a stampede—thundering suddenly and all at once. His temper operated the same way.

As far I could tell, the only time his pace stalled was during daily morning Mass. I only knew this because he had an early morning depo once and there wasn't enough time to go back to the office to get his trial briefcase after. So I carried it to him, the case and a large black umbrella, four blocks and up the steps of Our Lady of Perpetual Hope.

I watched him dip his nicotine-stained fingers into the holy water. Watched him kneel, hunched over the back of the pew like a deflated balloon, like Dali's melting pocket watch, and whisper to the Blessed Virgin for her guidance and forgiveness, a rosary laced between his fingers. I saw him scoot across the pew and walk to the altar head down, hands clasped. I saw him eat the body of Christ. I saw him drink Christ's blood. I saw his face bloom, the enraged creases of his forehead disappear.

After Communion, he didn't slide back into the pew. He nodded at me to follow. Once outside, he was desperate for a cigarette. He lit one with his gold lighter, an elaborate letter W engraved on the front.

He took a long drag, almost as if he were sucking the life back into himself.

After communion and the deposition, I trailed him back to the office where Verne was already tackling the work he put in her basket sometime after midnight. Wallenda looked over her shoulder. Irritated, he scowled. A nervous tick appeared in his jaw.

"Goddamn it, Verne. Why can't you ever set a pleading right?"

She never flinched or took her hands off her computer keyboard. Fingers working fast. "I'm not done yet, you asshole. Go have another cigarette and read your mail."

Ω

On the seventeenth floor, we had to break twice to procure band-aids for Preston's paper cuts. In my head, I could hear Wallenda say, "Little pussy."

I watched Preston roll the cuffs of his sleeves, exposing his forearms. His wrists were thick and strong. His veins meandered down the length of his arm and swelled to the surface of his tanned skin. My body remembered the press of his hips. The surge of warmth. I felt a thrill of prickled heat travel from the middle of my spine to the base of my neck. Anticipation. Longing. Regret. Preston, irresistible, with his swollen lip, the hint of a bruise, the crust of dried blood.

Jimmer in my head, "Why do you ruin everything? Why do you push everyone away?"

I didn't like it when Jimmer first came to live with us, the beautiful boy, the hand-me-down son of one of Dad's passing fancies. I resented Mom for loving him despite what he represented. Jimmer, such a sweet and troubled soul. Untamable, his teachers said. His brilliance complicated by bouts of depression and undiagnosed dyslexia. Mom taught him to read, found purpose in mending him, like an old woolen sock.

Margot adored him immediately. He was her pet. It was so much fun to have a brother in the family. Someone closer in age, someone to talk to about music and sex and drugs. They had secrets, spoke in code, tossed French phrases round the room. Eventually, I grew to love him too, in confusing, non-sisterly ways.

"I bet it was Mad Dog who told you about me, wasn't it?"

"Huh." Preston held a yellowed hand-written letter Bates stamped 678939997. He turned it this way and that trying to decipher the author's handwriting.

"Mad Dog?"

I could tell by the look on his face that I was right.

"How long you sp'ose this is gonna take?" Preston asked, heaving yet another box of engineering notes off the stacks. He checked his watch. "I was thinking maybe I could still make it to the Mudhen's? Or Tony Paco's? That's where everybody's going. After the baseball game."

"Tony Paco's? You're not missing much. I certainly wouldn't recommend the hot dogs. The only thing worth eating is the mashed potatoes and the meatloaf though they get a little carried away with the paprika."

Mom used to make meatloaf for Jimmer on his birthday. Always with baked potatoes and frozen acorn squash. I tried to make it for Jimmer and me last year. Right after I took the bar exam. I bought the pound of ground beef at Acme, mixed in a cup of Quaker Quick Oats, ketchup, Worcestershire sauce, and a dash of soy sauce. I cracked the egg on top of the mess. But I couldn't make myself plunge my hands into the bowl. I didn't want to feel Mom's love for Jimmer squish between my fingers.

I thought of Jimmer's Christmas tree and then I imagined smashing the thirteenth-floor window, tossing box after box after box, a flurry of memos fluttering down to the street below. Like that scene in *The Paper Chase* when the Harvard law student accidentally drops his property outline from his ivy-covered dorm room window, eight hundred pages, a year's worth of blood, sweat, and tears, his sole contribution to the study group, flying away.

"You should go," I said. "I'll keep looking for the letter and then I'll finish the memorandum to the court."

Preston grabbed his suit jacket.

"Are you sure?"

"What am I, your mother? Get the fuck out of here. Go eat some meatloaf and suck up to the partners. You'll be good at that."

The next morning, Wallenda called us both into his office. He waved the memorandum in the air. "Where's the fucking letter? How am I going to win the goddamn motion without the fucking letter?"

"I couldn't find it. I wrote the best argument I could without it," I said. I was dizzy from lack of sleep, too much coffee and vending machine sugar. I needed to brush my teeth and wash my face.

"You mean 'we' right? We couldn't find the letter?"

Preston shifted his feet, looked over at me. I didn't say anything. There was no reasoning with Wallenda when he got like this. Wallenda's hair fell into his eyes. He smoothed it back with his hand. Just before he threw the memo at Preston, aiming for his head.

"Get the fuck out my office," he said, and hurled a volume of *Ohio Rules of Civil Procedure* at him for good measure.

From far away, Jimmer whispered in my ear, "Say something." But Jimmer didn't know how these things worked. Preston was already toast. No way he'd get an offer now. I was already gathering the pages of the memorandum. I straightened their edges and handed it back to Wallenda.

"This memorandum that I wrote, with only two hours of sleep, is the best fucking argument you got. You're going to win the fucking motion."

Wallenda picked up a stapler, shook it at me like a mother wagging her finger at a naughty child, the thin line of his mouth, curling upward ever so slightly, then stapled the left-hand corner of the memorandum with a satisfying click.

TREVOR NEEDED A WIFE. Long before that late October morning, when the bar results came out, when he drank away the afternoon at Jukes, before the incident with Stash's green-chested bride. Long before he met the Banjo Man. He knew.

Some called the need a twitch, others a tingling, others still a burning. For Trevor, it was a rhythmic throbbing, an invisible pulse, an irrepressible dread that an essential part of himself was missing.

And in truth, it was. Mother took him to the doctor, as soon as she noticed it. After counting all his baby toes and fingers, she traced the nubs of his spine and then the blades of his chest, enumerating each rib over and over, fearing that she had lost count. The doctor said that, yes, while it was unusual, he acknowledged it happens, from time to time. A vast vacant space resided where the twenty-third and twenty-fourth ribs were supposed to float.

This was the story Mother told him the last time she thought she was dying. Stretched out on her divan, the crook of one arm dramatically flung over her face as if she had fainted, the other dangling off the side, fingertips trailing the depths of her shaggy mauve carpet. "I blame myself, of course, for your deformity." Trevor brought her a glass of water and her pills like he always did when she had one of her spells. Disappointed that she wouldn't be making pot roast for dinner. "Lord knows I've tried to make up for it." She sat up to take her medicine, tossed the handful back, followed it with a gulp of water. She was so thin, Trevor swore he could see the capsules travel down her throat. "But a mother's love can't make up for every deficiency. It's really just a band aid and this one is getting frayed at the edges." She placed her free hand on her heart. "We both must accept that I won't be around forever, taking care of you the way I do." *You mean hovering,* Trevor thought. He had always hated it, her meddling, her demands that he do this or that, the generosity of her checkbook contingent upon him performing like a little trained pet. "What will happen when the band aid gets ripped off?" Mother's hands trembled. Trevor took the glass from her and placed it on the coffee table, remembering to put a coaster underneath, just like he'd been taught.

With Mother's confession, suddenly, everything made sense, his anxieties and uncertainties, the confusion that came with sleepwalking through life. Until then, Trevor hadn't bought into that whole Adam's rib thing. But now he was certain that a wife was the only salve for his ache. That's when he promised Mother and himself that he'd propose to Jenny. Surely, Jenny would complete the puzzle—fill in the hole—where the missing ribs throbbed.

Nearly four years after he made that promise, he moped in a booth in the back corner of Jukes. His eyes bloodshot, ruby pink like the eyes of Jenny's albino rabbit, he wondered if he'd ever get married. Wondered if marriage would be like the long, last draw of the beer he'd been drinking: stale, bitter, flat. Or like the buzz he'd been nursing off and on all day: cloudy haze, shifting from light to dark. Or the jagged remnants of the expensive tie the bartender scissored in half. "Sorry man," he said as he tacked the yellow silk to the wall. "Rite of passage." Or perhaps it resembled the disco ball that hung ironically from the ceiling of Jukes, a sphere hanging by a thread, with a thousand tiny mirrors reflecting off the shiny faces of newly-minted lawyers and other smarmy types.

Earlier that morning, at five minutes to eight, just before he dialed the number for the bar results, Trevor downed his first shot of whiskey. His hands shook as he poured the second shot. "Fuck," he shouted as the amber liquid splashed onto his boxers and dribbled down into his dress socks, the black ones that pinched elastic circles into his calves.

He dialed six times before an electronic voice said, "Ohio Supreme Court, please hold."

He waited fifty-two minutes. He knew the long-distance charges would be astronomical.

At first he sat on the floral chintz loveseat—the one he'd bought for Jenny—straight backed, palms flat on his thighs, the phone cradled on his right shoulder. Despite his efforts to remain calm, his knees pumped up and down. He shifted the phone to the other shoulder. He did push-ups, then sit-ups. He jogged in place. He paced the floor as long as the olive green phone cord would allow. He slid open the balcony door, a swirl of leaves and cold air rushed in, and regarded the empty rabbit hutch where the rabbit, named Galvani's Nephew, used to live. A dog barked somewhere beyond the parking lot. The smell of frying bacon wafted up from the apartment below. He downed two more shots. One for Mother. One for Jenny.

And then finally, "Name please."

His ears burned. The missing ribs throbbed and stuttered. For a moment, he wasn't sure he'd get this answer right. "Trevor Ambrose? The third?"

He heard pages flipping, the voice coughed and then droned a dispassionate, "Passed."

He would have called Mother. But that last bout of dying turned out to be the real deal. He would have called Jenny. No, Jenny would have been there lying in his bed, their bed, wearing only his blue pinstriped oxford, smelling like sleep and apricot brandy, baby powder and sex. A wave of pink silk sheets spilling onto the floor. Or perhaps she'd be wrapped in their monogrammed towels, one around her body, the other, a turban, corralling her strawberry blonde hair. She would have called in sick. Together they would have plunged back into that silky pink sea. But there was no Jenny to celebrate with. Not anymore. "Now what?" he said to Mother, not sure whether to look up to the heavens or down below. He wrapped himself in the afghan Mother knitted so many years before, grabbed the whiskey bottle and ventured out onto his deck. Trevor crawled into the rabbit hutch, comforted by the faint ammonia smell, and sat for a while.

Ω

At Jukes, the celebration had been going all day. Big Dave shoulder-butted through the crowd of half-tanked baby lawyers with sawed-off ties. He halted abruptly in front of Trevor's booth. He carried a clutch of unopened bottles of beer in the crook of his left arm, two cans of Diet Coke in his left hand and an enormous plate of fries in his right.

"What's with the sour puss?" said Big Dave, unloading his burden with a clatter and clinks. Half of the fries slid onto the table which Big Dave scooped up with his massive paws and tossed back onto the plate. The red vinyl bench farted as he slid in opposite of Trevor. His bulk took up most of the two-person bench. Big Dave shoved all but the Diet Cokes and the fries in Trevor's direction.

"What's this?" said Trevor.

"Looks like I'm your designated Mother Goose for the day," he said pulling the tab on his pop. Big Dave slurped his Diet Coke, shoved a few fries into his mouth. "For the year actually. Supposed to mentor you, teach you shit like the importance of face time. Make sure you got everything you need. You know?" He salted the fries vigorously. Added a few shakes of pepper. He hulked over the table dipping his fries in a glob of ketchup. He shouted over the music, Wang Chung demanding *everybody have fun tonight*. "This is a big deal, Trev. Not everyone gets a Mother Goose. The partners have plans for you."

Trevor grabbed a beer. Raised it in salute.

Around five, the after-work crowd spilled into Jukes for happy hour. The lights dimmed, the disco ball spun into action. *Thriller* howled out of the juke box. Trevor and Big Dave surveilled the dance floor, watched the girls, the strobing arms and hips. Someone started a line dance.

Trevor, hypnotized by the winking lights, stared at Cissy Armstrong in her power suit, zombie clawing to Michael Jackson. Cissy was one third of the firm's trio of first years. She'd also passed the bar. Trevor burped. Acid burned his throat. He had hoped she would fail. He grabbed a handful of the bottle caps he'd been collecting, tossed one after the other in her direction, each missing their mark. Trevor wondered if she had been assigned a Mother Goose.

Big Dave laughed. "Don't even think about it. Strictly off limits," he said, nodding toward Cissy. "Besides, she's used goods. What you need is wife material. Don't you have some pretty little thing already snagged up?"

"Didn't work out." Trevor picked at the label on his beer then half-heartedly threw another bottle cap.

"Well, you've got to get back on the horse. Just not that one."

Trevor regarded Big Dave coldly. Surely Big Dave knew what had happened between him and Jenny. Didn't everyone?

Besides, Cissy wasn't his type. She looked ridiculous stomping and clapping, hips moving, pelvis thrusting, restricted by the cocoon of her suit. Her short hair slicked back like wet feathers. Her nose beakish. One side of her face appeared flat, almost smooshed, a sliver of a scar underlined her eye. The other side regaled a high cheekbone. As she pivoted from side to side, with every beat, she morphed from sparrow hawk to Russian princess.

So different from Jenny's slender nose that ski-sloped and ended with a kissable little button.

"Yep, a little missus will clean up this little side show you got going." Big Dave reached over and flipped Trevor's ragged tie. "Keep you in starched shirts, organize your sock drawer, take care of all those Christmas cards the firm expects you to send out. You know. Fast track you into the big tent. Who has time for seven, eight, nine years when you could make it in six, maybe five like me?"

Trevor nodded. He'd heard it all before. The partners wanted the associates hungry, clamoring for mortgages in Ottawa Hills and baby strollers in the back of their Dodge Caravans. Hamstered into producing more and more billable hours and making rain. And for those poor fucks who were too busy or too ugly—so much so that even the charm of a pedigree and a two-carat diamond couldn't do the trick—well, Trevor had heard, there were ways to get around all that dating before mating bullshit. Some sort of black swamp match-making voodoo the guys in the office whispered about.

Trevor twisted off the cap of an icy Michelob, wiped the opening with the remaining half of his tie. He thought about all that he had gained with that tiny word, *pass*. The next letter he dictated would be on newly engraved letterhead with "Trevor Ambrose, III" added to the top right-hand side under the list of associates. And every time he scrawled his signature at the end of correspondence or a pleading, he would add his newly acquired tail, "Esq." He could buy a new car and get a firm-sponsored membership to the City Gym and maybe even an invite someday to the Tile Club, a not-so-secret secret club of local visionaries, all male of course, who met weekly, ate steak, played cards, painted and conspired into existence cultural institutions such as the Toledo Art Museum. Trevor heard they also quietly shaped local politics and boosted careers of carefully curated young professionals.

But what did it all mean without Jenny and her silky satin sheets? He wanted the package deal, the two of them arm in arm at firm functions, over-the-top weekend getaways. He wanted to spend outrageous amounts of his salary on jewelry and Gucci handbags and her wicked little experiments. He wanted the partners to see her and know his worth.

Ω

Trevor and Jenny met in undergrad at BGSU when they were randomly assigned as lab partners in Bio 101. For Trevor the class was just a science requirement to get out of the way. For Jenny it was the dawn of her passion. In the drab brick box named Mosely Hall, which the students joked looked like an insane asylum, underneath the buzz of winking florescent lights, Trevor and Jenny dissected crayfish, frogs, and fetal pigs. Jenny, with her babydoll-pink nails, always did the cutting. She expertly used the forceps to pull back the exoskeleton or skin, poking around to find the organs, heart, liver, spleen, with each poke releasing a briny-sweet pickle smell. Once the TA examined Jenny's handiwork, she'd sever a limb, a pincer, a frog leg, a snout, and toss it into an empty drawer of their lab station. Trevor was horrified and oddly aroused by the growing collection. When Trevor asked, one day, why for fuck's sake did she always do that, she said, "I'm gonna Frankenstein me a perfect man. Care to offer up a part?" She glanced at his crotch. "In the interest of science, of course."

On the side, Jenny read books about Luigi Galvani and his studies on animal electricity. She invited Trevor to her dorm room to watch her reenact his experiments, goggles perched atop her strawberry blonde head, her dainty little hands clutching wires, connecting one end to a battery, the other to a pair of headless frog legs she'd stolen from the bio lab. One zap and the legs twitched like dancing zombies. The electric jolt startled Trevor's missing ribs.

Trevor proposed just before Jenny moved to Montreal for a scientific research fellowship at McGill and he left for law school in D.C. She looked dismayed when he took a knee until he produced a two-and-a-half carat brilliant cut diamond, financed by Mother of course. Three years passed, he graduated and then hermitted himself away in the spare bedroom of their new apartment to prepare for the bar exam.

Fueled by fear of failing, he studied constantly. Even in his sleep his mind rattled off the elements of murder, the tenets of property law, the four corners of a contract, the best interests of a child. He rebuffed Jenny's attentions, unmoved by her emerald green teddy. He refused to sleep in their bed, choosing instead the futon in the spare room, on account of his superstitions that sex would fuck with his brain. He rarely showered or shaved, lived on coffee by day and whiskey by night. Despite not eating much of anything, he acquired a little paunch.

Meanwhile, Jenny planned the wedding around the bar exam and his start date at Strathy, McMahon. She sampled hors d'oeuvres and chocolate truffle wedding cake, picked out bone China dinnerware, assembled her trousseau and conducted elaborate experiments on rabbit #243, the one she nicknamed Galvani's Nephew. Jenny hoped one day to take her experiments to the next level, just like Galvani's nephew, Giovanni Aldini, who aspired to reanimate human cadavers with sparks of electricity. Trevor felt bad for the little fella, took him out of his cage when Jenny wasn't looking. He loved his little nose, the way it twitched just like Jenny's when she was mad. His warm little body, when Trevor held him, eased Trevor's nerves.

Trevor didn't notice anything was amiss. Not even when he woke one night to find Jenny hovering above him, with jumper cables and a car battery in hand.

"What the fuck, Jenny?" Trevor scrambled to an upright position, grabbed Mother's afghan to cover his crotch.

Jenny smirked an impish grin, shrugged her shoulders. "Just trying to get a rise of out of you Trev. No biggie," she said. "Go back to sleep."

The last week of July, he drove to Columbus, sat for three days, Tuesday, Wednesday, Thursday, six hours a day, his number 2 pencil scribbling towards their future. It was worth it. His reward would be waiting for him. Friday, they'd rehearse and Saturday, they'd get married. He would be complete. His future secure.

Ω

Cissy broke away from the line, zombie stomped towards Trevor's table. Rotating disco ball mirrors and strobe lights flickered her progress like a slow-motion newsreel. She looked monstrous in her pleats and plaids and shoulder pads. Trevor couldn't imagine anyone desiring the Russian hawk; it couldn't possibly be true what they said about her. But then, that's what he had thought about Jenny. Trevor remembered Preston, one of the summer associates, talking about the time he kissed Cissy in the Toledo Edison Building, in the war room. How she bit his lip.

Cissy shouted over the din of music and bar chatter, "Hey, Trevor Three Sticks." She slapped his shoulder like they were old friends and grabbed the longneck he'd been holding. She didn't even bother wiping the mouth of bottle before tilting it back and guzzling the remainder of his beer. She handed it back. "We're big swinging dicks now. You ready to go to Stash's for the Esquire Ball?"

He remembered that Preston said she bit so hard his lip bled. Trevor thought he imagined the taste of blood until he realized that his own lip was bleeding. He pressed a cocktail napkin to his mouth, it came back red.

Trevor took a few deep breaths, thought about the untimely death of Jenny's white rabbit, calmed the need growing inside him, and stood as he tried to ignore his phantom limb. As he staggered out the door, he thought heard Big Dave say, "You need to see the Banjo Man."

Ω

Mr. and Mrs. Ashe lived over in Maumee in a grand three-story brick house with black shutters and a red door framed by a columned portico. Despite the large house, Mrs. Ashe loved to spend most of her time outdoors. Unlike their prim and proper street side with its obligatory mounds of yellow and burnt orange mums, the backyard was a riot of animal topiaries, twinkle lights, and tiki torches. Beyond the fire pit and the gazebo, the lawn stretched several acres towards the woods and a little creek that trickled into the Maumee River. Having been a wet summer and warm fall, the perimeter of rose bushes still boasted cabbage-sized blooms. The trees clung to their golden leaves. Sweet autumnal rot mixed with smoke and the smell of burning logs. Every so often a twig would spark and an ember would pop and float into the air.

Mr. Ashe became a partner with Strathy, McMahon sometime back in the seventies. His practice consisted of mild-mannered estate planning, wills and trusts and financial vehicles designed to avoid inheritance tax. He didn't have the Strathy, McMahon look. Small in stature, he was also a bit on the frail side, with thinning brown hair and an absurd mustache, which he twirled into Dali-esque curls. Despite his timid demeanor, he was wildly successful; his associates billed and billed, while his collectibles skyrocketed. And so, when people referred to him as "The Stash," it was out of veneration rather than ridicule.

Stash's wife was of unknown origin. One day Stash was single, the next he was married to a woman with an indescribable hue.

Some people thought maybe she was from Cincinnati or Steubenville. Others thought perhaps she hailed from Louisiana given her love for swamp music.

Every fall, just before Halloween, once the Supreme Court released the bar exam results, Stash's wife hosted the Esquire Ball. Initially, it was a small gathering for the firm, but gradually it grew to include other law firms and professionals from Big Ag, local banks, shipping concerns, companies that manufactured glass and elevators.

Back at Jukes, Cissy wrestled away Trevor's keys, insisted they drive together in his car, insisted she knew how to drive a stick, but the grinding, the lurching back and forth as Cissy shifted the gears, said otherwise. By the time they arrived, found a place to park down the street, Stash's backyard swarmed with suits, their wives draped like strings of pearls, ornaments later banished to the koi pond to admire the swans, the floating gardenias and lily pads. Top-hatted waiters decked out in waistcoats and green velvet tails offered trays of champagne and canapes and imported cigars. Cissy grabbed a Montecristo and marched off, her heels sinking into the grass, to join a gaggle of old paunchy men puffing away in a conspiratorial circle.

Later, Trevor would remember that this was the point where time began to bend backwards and forwards. Dizzy from the day drinking, the strobe lights, *Thriller* throbbing in his ears, Cissy's driving, he grabbed an open bottle of Dom Perignon and snaked his way through the various clusters of revelers. He had his eye on the elegant weeping willow beyond the koi pond and fire pit. He picked a spot under the tree next to the stream. The ground was damp, so he spread out his suitcoat and leaned against its trunk. The drooping branches curtained him from the crowd like a bridal veil.

For the first time since he returned from Columbus back in July, weary, sleep-deprived, unshaven, dehydrated and shaking from too much caffeine, but triumphant, certain he had passed the bar and ready to claim Jenny as his prize, he fully submitted to his folly, his deep unwavering need for Jenny but his even stronger love for his brilliant future, the seeds for his ultimate humiliation.

Ω

Trevor was confused when the keys to his apartment no longer turned the tumblers of the lock. He knocked at first and then pounded on the door.

Jenny peered through the crack, then stepped out, shielding from his view what he guessed must be her wedding gown, just beyond the stacks of early wedding gifts wrapped in silver and white and lavender. He couldn't wait to see her walk down the aisle, to show her off. His beautiful little bunny with her beautiful little bunny nose. The whole firm was invited. It was an unspoken Strathy, McMahon rule. Jenny was a little irritated about the expanding guest list. Snapped that her parents couldn't afford to feed all those lawyers. She relented when he opined that he had no one else to invite. Without Mother, the firm was the only family he had.

"You changed the lock?"

"Had to, someone broke in. Galvani is missing."

"No, no he's not. He's down in the car with the rest of my stuff."

"What the hell, Trevor. You stole Galvani's Nephew?"

"Come on, babe. You know me. He's my lucky rabbit's foot."

Trevor reached for her elbow, then leaned in for a kiss.

She turned her head, pushed him away.

"You stink," she said.

It was true. He had overslept the last morning of the exam. He'd packed up his things, checked out of the hotel and raced to the Convention Center without shaving or taking a shower. He might have also been nipping on a flask of bourbon on the way home.

Trevor noticed for the first time that Jenny was dressed in her bathrobe.

"You getting ready to go out?"

She shook her head. A swath of lace from the peignoir she'd bought for their honeymoon peeked out. She pulled the robe tighter.

"What's going on here?" He grabbed her wrists but she twisted away. She turned to shut the door in his face. He clawed her back, pulling off her robe in the process. "Is someone in there? In our bed?"

"I was going to tell you. But first your mom died, then it was finals, then graduation and then you were studying for this god-damn-fucking-three-day-marathon of an exam. I couldn't do it."

Without thinking, Trevor balled up his fist. Jenny's face flushed. "I'm not going to hit you. You're not worth it," he yelled, surprised by his reaction. He felt a momentary surge of power. He was the one in charge after all.

The neighbors in 2C and 2D flung open their doors and peered into the hallway.

"Oh. I'm worth it, Trevor," Jenny said. She yanked off her night-gown revealing her small ripe breasts, her translucent flesh, her soft little belly. The secret place that he would never enter. "Take a look everyone. Aren't I worth it?" She wadded up the bathrobe and nightie, throwing them at Trevor, then turned to expose her heart-shaped ass as she slid back into the apartment, clicked the door shut. Trevor heard the deadbolt thunk.

Later, he would take Jenny's albino rabbit, Galvani's Nephew, wring its neck and throw it into the dumpster behind Tony Packo's. The one over on Front Street.

Trevor didn't cry that night. He didn't cry when he told the firm that the wedding had been called off. He didn't cry after he cleared Jenny out of the apartment and returned the wedding gifts. He hadn't cried any of the sixty days since. Not until the Esquire Ball, choking down hundred-dollar gulps of champagne. This is how Stash's wife found him. Sobbing uncontrollably underneath her willow tree.

Ω

The next day, the day after the Esquire Ball, the summons arrived by courier. The receptionist called Trevor to the front desk to sign for it. He had been hiding in his office all morning, venturing out into the hallway only once to retrieve a cup of coffee and a glass of water to down a handful of baby aspirin he found in the seventeenth floor kitchen. Now, he studiously stared at the yellow legal pad he carried, pretending to be deep in thought rather than obviously avoiding eye contact with any passersby. His humiliation dragged his shoulders forward into a remorseful slump. The fluorescent light hum followed him down the too-bright corridor, burrowing deep, first into his ear then nestling somewhere next to the dull thumping in his brain. He pushed open the heavy oak doors into the heartbeat of the firm, the oval reception area. He expected to see a helmeted delivery guy, bicycle wheel clutched under his left armpit, rolled pant leg cinched with a rubber band and hairy leg slick with mud splatter. Instead, he was met by a brown-suited ancient, white muttonchops caressing the folds of his wizened face, bald headed except for the fringe of white fluff—a furry Saturn ring—encircling his skull. The man held out a silver tray as if he were a butler serving tea.

"Trevor Ambrose, the third," he said pausing to emphasize, "Esquire?"

Startled to hear his title for the first time, Trevor nodded yes.

The man urged the tray forward, "Sign here, please, Mister Ambrose."

Trevor plucked the ecru-colored pouch off the tray, signed the ledger, and stumbled back to the safety of his office. The foil-lined envelope engraved with gold calligraphy resembled a wedding invitation. With trembling hands, Trevor tore it open to find yet another envelope hidden behind a slim square of tissue paper. Before he could unnest the remainder of the package, Cissy knocked on the door.

"Busy?"

She didn't wait for a response. She flounced in and flopped into his guest chair. Trevor slid the envelope underneath a file folder.

"What's this?" she said grabbing a pickle jar off his desk, holding it up to the light. She shook it, slimy green muck clouded the water.

"Hey!" Trevor grabbed for the jar, but Cissy pulled it close to her chest. "Come on—give me that. What are we in sixth grade?" he said.

"What is it? A souvenir from last night?"

"Why are you here, Cissy?"

Cissy swirled the green slime before relinquishing the jar. "I wanna know why I'm the one everyone is whispering about when you're the guy who got shitfaced and passed out in Stash's backyard," she said. "I mean, where's the crime in smoking a cigar?"

Trevor pressed his palm into his right eye, trying to stop its thrumming.

Cissy picked at her tongue, flicking into the air remnants of cigar paper and tobacco from the night before. She folded her arms, crossed her right leg over the left, pumped it ferociously, so fast he thought her black patent pump would rocket off her foot.

Trevor heard the anger splinter in the back of her throat. She looked away. He contemplated the visible curve of her face, the hawk side momentarily vulnerable, a side he hadn't pondered before, almost pretty in its sadness. For a moment Trevor felt sorry for her. But what did she expect? Insisting her way in. Sucking on a cigar, a brown Cuban cock. For all to see. To what end? What was she trying to prove?

"Do you even remember what happened last night?" she said.

Of course he did. Bluegrass music twanging. All the beautiful women on display. Roving waiters tipping their black satin hats.

Then someone asked, "Hey, aren't you the guy who brought his fiancé's rabbit to the Convention Center—to the bar exam? Why'd you do that?"

Trevor wondered how to respond and then said, "Well, it was too hot to keep it in the car."

How could he explain that he had stolen Galvani's Nephew, one, to save it from the barbarous experiments Jenny performed at the lab, and two, because it calmed his nerves, made him less neurotic, made him miss her less.

"How is she?"

"The rabbit?"

"No, your fiancé—your wife?"

His wife, the rabbit. The two were inseparable in his brain. Maybe he hadn't tossed it in the dumpster. Perhaps he left it on Tony Packo's doorstep in a basket like a baby? Perhaps Tony, himself, sautéed it in garlic and sweet paprika then stewed it with tomatoes and brown sugar into Hungarian goulash. Or maybe rabbit paprikash? Perhaps he just took him to a park, let the little fella scamper out into the tangle of grasses and thorny weeds.

That's when he grabbed the champagne and slumped away.

The willow tree seemed to beckon him, lazily waving its delicate arms in the breeze. He found comfort in the way the music and the laughter of the partygoers faded. He became aware of crickets, a swelling chorus of cicadas, trickling water. An owl hooting. The pluck of a banjo string. Swamp music.

And when Stash's wife parted the curtains of the weeping willow's branches, looking like an angel fabricated from sea glass, the low-slung moon behind her, a halo.

"Are you an angel?" he said.

"No," she said, "but you look like you could use one." Her voice had a lovely lilting quality, softly British.

She had brought a tiki torch to light the way. She plunged it into the damp ground outside the willow's protective bonnet. She squatted next to him. Pried the bottle of Dom from his hands.

"Tell me, Darling," she said, draping her arm across his shoulders. "Tell me all about it."

So he did. Everything. Even about Jenny's rabbit. Even about what he'd done to it. She cradled him in her arms, as he rested his head against her iridescent bosom. She twirled his hair with her long proby fingers, twisting the ends into curlicues. Every once in a while, he felt the flick of a tongue on his temple like the comforting lick of a dog.

He rubbed her back. Round circular motions. She felt so fragile. Underneath the citrine, gauzy fabric of her dress, he could feel every tiny bone, every ripple of skin. The absence of a bra. His fingers detected two ridges, like vertical ribs, on either side of her spine. His phantom limb ached. The swamp music swelled and gave him courage. Trevor leaned in to kiss her, Mr. Stash's wife.

She kindly refused. "Oh no. I'm sorry, Darling, but it is awfully sweet of you to think of me in that way."

Her gentle rebuff sent him howling into the rubbery softness of her chest. She pulled him up to a standing position. All he wanted to do was sleep. He laid his head on her green shoulder.

"Come on now, Darling. It's time to visit the Banjo Man."

She held his hand, leading the way, far from the Esquire Ball, following the creek until it trickled into a wide stream. They hopped onto a lily pad. Using the tiki torch to pole their skiff, she pushed away from the bank, propelled them forward, steering clear of smashed beer cans. A large carp followed, its sad downturned mouth opening and closing in menacing protest. Stash's wife jabbed at it with her torch until he swam away. The stream picked up speed, raced down a foamy waterfall of lichen and rocks, reminding Trevor of the time he went white water rafting at Ohio Pyle with his Boy Scout troop.

Stash's wife snacked on flies along the way, her long magnificent tongue flicked into the swampy air snapping up mosquitoes, moths, and dragonflies. With each gulp her eyes rolled back into a dreamy ecstasy. Trevor marveled at the efficiency of her agile tongue and sticky saliva. He thought about Christmas cards, all of those envelopes and stamps that had to be licked. He thought about Mr. Stash. The lucky bastard.

After what seemed like ages, they floated into a large cement sewer pipe. In the distance, Trevor could see the outline of a tall, stickish man. He heard the twang of a banjo string.

Ω

Trevor opened a case book, flipped through his legal pad, collected highlighters into a tidy fist, clicked his pen, hoping Cissy would get the hint to leave. He stared at the page without seeing the words. He could hear Jenny saying, "You are so passive aggressive."

"You've got to be kidding me," Cissy said. She snatched at the envelope he had hidden under his books. "YOU got invited to the Tile Club? Already? Doesn't someone have to die first?"

She got up to leave in a huff.

"Why are you so mad? They don't let girls in anyway."

Cissy slammed the door on the way out.

Ω

The Tile Club was located on 13th Street between Monroe and Jefferson. The invitation directed him to arrive at five PM. Trevor figured it was a twenty-minute walk from SeaGate Tower. He didn't want anyone to know that he was leaving early, so he planned a stealthy escape via the emergency stairwell. Normally, he would have tidied his office, closed his casebooks, stacked files, turned off his banker's lamp. Instead, he left his desk with two splayed volumes of Corpus Juris Secundum, legal pads, a scatter of sticky notes and highlighters, a full mug of coffee, and an opened bag of cheese doodles. He left his overcoat draped on the arm of a guest chair and his briefcase on the seat. He turned on his little transistor radio with the volume low. Everything appeared as if he just stepped out for a moment.

It was Halloween, already getting dark. Trevor wondered, as he descended the seventeen floors, if there would be any trick-or-treaters at his apartment, wondered if he should stop at the grocery store and buy a few bags of candy. There didn't seem to be many kids in his building, just a chubby little boy surely too big for a pacifier, but one stuffed in his mouth all the time, nonetheless. And a pretty little girl who wore a sparkly pink tutu over her jeans and carried a headless, naked Barbie doll. She reminded him of Jenny.

He thought about last year. How Jenny came to visit. They carved pumpkins, toasted the seeds, filled his popcorn bowl full of Tootsie rolls and lollipops. He bought a cassette tape of spooky music, played it on the boom box they set by the front door. For a kick, they put on costumes. Jenny dressed up like a mad scientist. Trevor like a bunny.

The weather had turned sometime during the day. Gone were the warm summerlike breezes from the night before. The temperature must have fallen thirty degrees since morning. The truth of it shocked him when he opened the emergency exit door and stepped out into twilight. As he turned the corner, a gust of wind nearly knocked him off his feet. Random pages of newspaper and litter swirled at his feet. An icy mist stung the back of his neck. He pulled up his suit collar, pushed his way forward, pacing his steps to the music of the city buses, honking horns and one lousy muffler that dogged him all the way to Monroe.

13th Street was a solid sea of concrete sidewalks and vacant lots except for one modest row house. A flank of chipped brick was the only evidence that other houses once hugged its sides. Trevor hesitated, took a deep breath before mounting the four steps of the front stoop. He used the brass lion's head knocker to announce his arrival.

Rafferty, the same old gent who delivered the invitation, opened the door to the Tile Club.

"Welcome, welcome Mr. Ambrose. So glad you could visit on such short notice. Come on in and get out of that nasty premonition of things to come."

Rafferty, stoop-shouldered but dandy in a red sweater vest, argyle tie and charcoal gray suit jacket, led the way into the great room just off the entry. He had the look of a man once tall and commanding, possibly cruel, softened, lessened by age. He motioned toward the brick fireplace.

"You can thaw out while I prepare the guest book."

Trevor surveyed the room as he warmed his hands. A nineteenth century portrait of a mutton-chopped, deeply-jowled titan of industry glared down from his perch over the mantel. Crude wrought iron implements leaned on the hearth ready to stoke the embers of a fire. The room smelled stale like an antique store. The clear-headedness Trevor had acquired from the walk over quickly faded among the musty, mildewed room. From floor to ceiling, oils, watercolors, and lithographs, some quite good, some sadly amateurish, crammed the wide plank oak paneling. Rivulets furrowed and rutted the panels. Trevor pressed his fingertips into the trailed grooves, wondered what made them.

Rafferty, suddenly beside him, pulled on a pair of white gloves. "That would be the ghost of corn and wheat from the old grain elevator," he said, explaining that years of grain pouring into the silo caused the striations. The planks were salvaged after a fire and repurposed by the Tile Club. He handed a pair of gloves to Trevor. "You'll need these to sign the guest book."

Rafferty presented the dusty old ledger, ninety-some years old and fifty pounds from the looks of it. It lay open on a rickety lectern.

"You know, I was here the first time the members brought this register out to be signed. Everyone who visits puts his John Hancock in there, one way or another." He flipped to the front of the book, landing on a page of handsome hunting dogs, sketched in pencil. "Edmund Henry Osthaus. German gent. Became a member in 1896."

Rafferty leafed back to the first page, pointed to David Stine's signature, 1895.

"Ever heard of him?"

Trevor shook his head.

"He's the founding member of this place. The architect of his day. Designed some fine houses over on the West End. Couple of schools. And the county courthouse. Had a thing about frogs. There's a tile mosaic in the rotunda. And, outside of the building? Covered with sandstone frogs."

Trevor began to sweat. He could smell the alcohol from the night before leaching from his pores, mixing with the Tile Club dust. He could smell the decay.

"Care to have a look?"

Trevor didn't but he politely turned the fragile, yellowed pages forward until he found one that looked like field notes from a biology experiment.

"More frogs, I'm afraid."

Indeed. Headless torsos of frogs jigged across the paper into the folds of the spine. A flash of wild-eyed Jenny, gloved hands, clutching wires, connecting one end to a battery, the other to the pair of frog legs. The familiar ache of his phantom limb.

Trevor tugged at that space just above the knot of his tie, loosening the grip of his white button-down Oxford.

Rafferty flipped forward to where the last entry had been made.

"So. Are you ready to sign, Mr. Ambrose?" He offered a Mont Blanc pen for the task. Trevor scratched his name on the designated line, capped the pen, overwhelmed by an impending sense of doom.

"Where are the others?" Trevor said handing back the pen.

"Oh well, David, I believe you know him. He's with your firm. He's back in the kitchen preparing the steaks—he'll be grilling them in the fireplace later. Ever have fire-grilled steaks?"

Again, Trevor shook his head.

"Smithers, he's an accountant. He's making the cowboy coffee. The rest of them are up there with the artist types and the musical guest for the night. Setting up their easels and paint brushes, no doubt."

Out of the great room into the hall, Trevor studied the garrison of portraits of white men in suits, some realistic, some folksy and primitive.

"Hope you can sit still for an hour or two," Rafferty said nodding to the nearest row of badly painted oils. "You're next."

Trevor wondered why, but did not ask. He followed Rafferty up the steep and narrow steps. More pictures lined the way. Trevor bumped one with his shoulder. He felt the frame, along with his heart, sway back and forth before settling back into position. He envisioned a cascade of landscapes and flowers and sour-faced sentinels dominoing down the stairway onto the floor below. Suddenly, he became aware of clamoring, jovial voices. He and Rafferty spilled into the large open expanse of the studio.

"Ah, there you are Rafferty, you old bag o' bones. And young Mr. Ambrose, I presume?"

An equally wizened owl ambled over and pulled off his round wire-rimmed glasses. He wiped them clean with his green striped tie and put them back on before offering his hand.

"John Castleton's the name, Toledo Trust." A green silk hanky peeked out his breast pocket. Castleton offered him a drink. "Some of us are beholden to our gin and tonics, but you look like a Scotch man to me." Castleton handed Trevor a tulip-shaped snifter, poured the amber liquid from a crystal decanter. Notes of tobacco, smoke, and old leather mixed with peat drifted up, filling his brain with a memory that he couldn't quite capture.

Soon Trevor was surrounded by a gaggle of old men waving paint brushes, clinking glasses, slapping his back and shaking hands. They inquired after his admission to the bar, the date of the swearing in, his plans for Strathy, McMahon. Trevor started to enjoy himself.

Then Stash walked in. Trevor hadn't known he was a Tiler.

"STASH," the gents chorused.

"It's about time Mr. Ambrose took the stage. Shall we proceed to our easels, gentlemen?"

Mr. Ash ushered Trevor to a carved armchair centered on a raised platform, a gray sheet lazily tacked to the back wall drooped in swooshes serving as a backdrop. Stash's mustache waxed into an upward flourish. He smiled, revealing a set of yellowish crooked teeth.

"I understand you spent some time with my wife last night."

Adrenalin burbled up Trevor's spine and settled at the base of his neck.

"You do understand why you are here, do you not? You realize the invitation to join us is highly unusual?"

Trevor's head hurt.

"Take a sip of your drink. That will help you remember."

Trevor sat in the chair, sipped Scotch from the glass tulip. He tasted dirt and seaweed. Earth filled with moss and tree roots and decay.

Trevor looked out into the sea of paintbrushes. Seeing for the first time, his Mother Goose, Big Dave.

"What's going on here?"

Then he remembered. The sewer pipe, the banjo twang.

Ω

"This is where I leave you, Darling," said Mrs. Stash.

Trevor stepped off the lily pad into the shock of ankle-deep water penetrating his oxblood wingtips. His socks slurped up the seepage like a straw. Mrs. Stash fluttered her lovely green fingers. He watched as she floated away, upstream until she disappeared into the late evening fog. Trevor sloshed onward, towards the pipe's end. Towards the Banjo Man.

The Banjo Man struck a match, briefly illuminating the funny looking instrument strapped to his chest, a banjo made of gourds and goat skin. A moss-colored fedora dipped low onto his forehead. A joint dangled from his slanty, lipless mouth. Trevor didn't smoke but took a drag when offered, coughing between hits. It tasted like dirt and baseball mitt with notes of licorice and forgotten bones.

Side by side, they trudged out of the pipe and into a brook that faded into a mucky trench bordered with cattails and swamp grass.

Trevor couldn't see but could smell the wetland ooze, decomposing debris, fecund earth protesting under his ruined leather soles. Fermented, womblike, the metallic smell of fertile expectation. Fishy, yeasty, molasses. Like the rotting possibilities hidden deep within Tony Packo's dumpster. Trevor imagined a scurry of river rats and snakes and slimy salamanders, set to the music of crickets and a hooting owl.

Trevor's wingtips skidded, his socks squelched, his feet pruned. He tripped over roots. The Banjo Man pushed through a thicket of branches which swung back and hit Trevor in the face. Eventually they reached a clearing.

A campfire blazed. Smoke from peat and moss and dried leaves circled the encampment.

"It's about time you got here," said a familiar voice. It was Big Dave.

"Mother Goose!" Trevor shouted with relief. The others stood, each in turn shook his hand. Partners from the firm. The headliners Strathy and McMahon. Mr. Stash. A man named Rafferty offered cowboy coffee from a white enamel pot.

Big Dave threw a slab of meat into the fire. The flesh burned and sizzled. The smell was both horrid and mouth-watering.

The Banjo Man stood off to the side. Smoking another joint.

"Why am I here?" Trevor said. He scratched his head, looked from face to face.

"Don't you know?" said Stash. He lit his cigar, puffed robustly until the end produced a red glow.

"Um, no."

"I thought you were here for a wife. After all, mine is no longer available." Stash looked menacing in the moonlight. The others laughed.

"Don't worry, son," said Rafferty patting him on the back. "Folks are always clamoring after Stash's wife. So that's why you're here. To get a wife of your own."

"Here?"

"Why, certainly. The finest spot in the county. No better place than out in the swamp, a hearty fire and cigars to keep the black flies away, the chorus of crickets and other critters and the twang of banjo strings to stir things up." He nodded to the Banjo Man. "Play us some of that clawhammer, Guy."

The Banjo Man pushed up his hat, swung his banjo from his back to his front. Trevor thought of that scene in Deliverance. Instead of "Dueling Banjos," the Banjo Man plunked one string, slow, offbeat, out of tune. Mournful. He wailed, like an Appalachian miner, a songful poem, "When Sorrow Encompasses Me."

Every man around the campfire had tears in his eyes. Stash handed Trevor an empty pickle jar with holes punched into the tin lid. "Here you go, Son."

"I don't understand," Trevor said.

"Go to the stream, scoop yourself up some candidates that the Banjo Man called forth."

Trevor still didn't understand but did as he was told. He scooped up a jar full of water and muck that he'd just waded through. He screwed on the lid and wandered back over to the fire.

"Let's see how you did. Hold 'er up to the light."

Trevor held up the jar. The mud sank to the bottom and one little tadpole swam through the gunk.

"Why there she is," Stash said. "Raise her up right, now

Ω

After the Tilers painted his portrait, after he gorged on the dinner of nothing but chimney-charred steaks with dripping bloodred centers, after all the backslapping, predictions of his bright future, after Trevor agreed that his helpmeet (the Tilers were fond of Genesis 2:18—the King James version), a little green woman at home would cement his success, after Trevor promised to keep them informed as to his upcoming nuptials, to invite them all, he was dismissed into the frigid, moonless night. It was sleeting. Tiny shards of ice hit his face.

Stunned, Trevor stumbled back to Portside and SeaGate Tower, wondering what it all meant. Was it all an elaborate ruse? Hazing? A fucking practical joke? The Tilers never actually mentioned anything about frog wives, did they? When they combined the word "green" with "woman" maybe they meant one that was inexperienced, pliable? And what to do about the half-formed amphibian swimming in a little jar in his office? He didn't know how to raise frogs or wives. Maybe he should call Jenny? They hadn't spoken in months but maybe she'd agree to talk to him in the interest of science? Or maybe Mrs. Stash. Surely, she knew what to do. Were there schools? Lessons in dancing, flower arranging, calligraphy? Deportment, and charm? Were there governesses for such things? He imagined Mrs. Stash arriving with a parrot-headed umbrella and a large carpet bag, a stern but kind countenance and a long list of must-dos for training the perfect wife.

Back at Strathy, McMahon, he strode past the night receptionist without saying hello, ignored the stack of pink message slips she waived at him. As he neared his office, he heard the fuzzy static and intermittent whine from his AM radio that had lost its signal after sunset. And of course there was Cissy lurking in his doorway, arms loaded with a fat redwell stuffed with pleadings from the nuclear power plant case, two volumes of *Corpus Juris Secundum* that he had been using. His bag of cheese puffs topped the stack. No surprise there. She was always hungry. Cissy's hunger was embarrassing. And selfish. And intoxicating.

"What the hell Cissy?" he said, smoothing back his wet hair with his palm.

"Wallenda waits for no one, thus neither do I," she said tartly. Then she wrinkled her brow and glared at him. "You were probably one of those guys in law school that hid the casebooks, right? Or maybe you just tore out the relevant pages? Well, we're all on the same team here. So don't be a book hog, Trev. And don't be mad at me for borrowing the ones I need."

"I don't give a shit about the books but stealing my cheese puffs? That takes a lot of nerve."

"I traded you some licorice."

"The licorice that you borrowed," he said, using air quotes, "from the law librarian's reference desk?" He snatched the bag, which was nearly empty. Orange crumbs lingered on Cissy's mouth. Crumbs which he had the sudden urge to lick off. "Out!" he shouted and pointed down the hallway.

"Sheesh," she said as she left.

He fiddled with the knob on his radio until he found a remarkably clear station in Baton Rouge playing Cajun Creole and started to pack up his briefcase. He neatened his desk for the night, noted that Cissy, that liar, had failed to leave her trade. Arranged his yellow highlighters just so. The watermark on his desk surprised him because he always used coasters. It was then that he realized that his pickle jar was missing. "Cissy," he growled. She was such a menace. He marched to her office.

"You took her, didn't you?"

"What?"

"You fucking stole her!"

"What are you talking about?" she said biting off the end of a black Twizzler.

"My, my…" *My wife*, he said to himself, *you stole my beautiful, slimy, talented frog wife who I hadn't had the chance to train yet, my lady frog in waiting, my success…my missing rib, my helpmeet, my fast track to partner.* "My tadpole."

Cissy covered her mouth trying not to laugh. "Oh my god Trev, you are a total nut job." She waggled the Twizzler at him. Trevor reached across the desk, knocking over a tower of casebooks and file folders in the process, grabbed the licorice and shouted, "Mine!"

Drive

LAST NIGHT I DREAMT I WENT TO BAVARIA AGAIN. Zooming the autobahn with the Captain, windows down, my long brown hair whipping away the hot sun, I thrilled as he shifted the gears. With no speed limit, the Captain, handsome and rugged in his army fatigues, pushed his American car, the one he shipped over for his tour of duty, past seventy-five, then eighty inching toward eighty-five, eighty-six, eighty-seven until it shuddered violently. He laughed at me as I clutched the grab handle above the door. He loved to torture me this way, to drive me to the brink. Eventually, he eased off the gas, won me over with a wink. Meanwhile the German cars, the Audis, the BMWs, the Volkswagens sped past, so fast as if we were standing still as time flashed forward.

It seemed to me we were living a fairytale, as we motored the *Romantische Strasse*, a route dreamed up by travel agents in the fifties, past tidy farms, over rolling hills and through the forest where enchanted creatures lurked. With the Captain, a whole new world opened up to me, while the ancient moss-covered trees, and the edges of the Bavarian Alps closed in behind us, barring our return trip back to Ansbach, to the military base where I processed Article 15 letters of reprimand, non-judicial punishments for private first class dumb-assery: nights of drunken debauchery, failing to show up for duty on time, mouthing off, or just doing a shitty job. On the road, memories of my dull attic apartment in the boxy concrete house on the hill, a steep, thirty-three step climb up from Richard Wagner Strasse, faded away.

A few days earlier, the Captain found me on the corner staring at a handful of pfennigs and a solitary Deutschmark, before Euros were a thing, daring myself to approach a little sausage cart. I'd been in country for weeks and I was starving. Starving because, other than the lunches I ate on base, buttery triangles of grilled cheese and French fries, I consumed little else, too timid, given my limited German vocabulary, to visit the Aldi or even that corner stand, next to one of those ubiquitous cigarette machines that looked like newspaper boxes. I longed to order a crusty roll—*ein bratwurst mit senf*—and the orange cola drink called Spezi. Mostly, I was starving for my life to begin. To reinvent myself.

Back home in Ohio, I left behind a honeycomb of boys I needed: boys for coffee, boys for dinner, boys for transportation, boys for fixing things, boys for advice. Their short-vowelled Midwestern accents seemed quaint compared to the Captain's square-jawed New York City assertions. Instead of helping me, the Captain encouraged me to speak up, to order for myself. He nudged me, his shoulder playfully bumping into mine. *C'mon, I know, you can do it.* He said I reminded him of Angela from the neighborhood back on Staten Island. The girl next door with skinned knees and lopsided braids. Everyone's little sister. *Except now she's a fox busting balls on Wall Street.*

We sat in lime green café chairs on the sidewalk outside the *apotheke*. In between bites, and the Captain handing me a napkin to wipe the mustard off my chin, I told him that I was with the JAG Corps, just for the summer, and then back to the States for my second year of law school. The Captain took a swig of my Spezi. He told me about the company of young soldiers he commanded, mostly in the field, how their sole mission was to stare into the eyes of the communists across the border. He'd be heading out again soon, didn't know when he'd be back. He asked me where else I'd been since arriving at the airport in Frankfurt. *Nowhere,* I said. *Just here.* It hadn't occurred to me to that I could travel anywhere else. Within hours of our meeting, I agreed to go away with him to see what else there was to see.

We spent the night in a castle hotel, our room a crumbling medieval turret. In the midst of all that decay, we enjoyed a tender preamble, the Captain inquiring sweetly *is this okay? Are you sure?* And *how about this? And this? And this?* The Captain waited patiently for my whispered, kittenish permissions until I lost myself to him, to the moment, eager to fill myself with possibilities. The Captain was a bear of a man, the weight of him consumed me, the stubble on his chin scratched then burned my face, his enormous paws mauled my flesh. After the pain of all that pleasure, he fell into a long deep sleep; and I, sad and lonely, knowing there were no happily-ever-afters, sat in the castle's deep window well and gazed out the ancient mullioned windows. A raven pecked at the latch.

The Captain knew the castle breakfast buffet of cold meats, cheeses, muesli, and yogurt wouldn't satisfy my hunger for long. He stuffed several prepackaged squares of pumpernickel bread into my pockets for later. We drove to Rothenburg ob der Tauber, a medieval village overlooking the river. I was charmed by the half-timbered gingerbread houses with pointed gables, red tiled roofs, and blooming flower boxes. In the *altstadt*, we walked the walls and climbed the towers that fortified the old city. We strolled the cobblestoned marketplace, kissed a tender lingering kiss in front of the crooked yellow house, the famous one, with teal shutters at the fork in the road. We mingled with the eager tourists in the cuckoo clock shop. We explored the gothic St. James Church, gasped at its cathedral ceiling. The Captain genuflected before the ornately carved Holy Blood Alter which purportedly held a crystal reliquary of Christ's blood. I admired his modest reverence, wished I could summon some of my own, wished I could create a space for something, anything, to believe in.

Back on the street, I unwrapped my pumpernickel bread, dropping crumbs as we wandered. We happened upon a human-sized wrought iron bird cage, forged centuries before, suspended in the air by a long metal arm. It looked like the one the old witch used to imprison Hansel, to fatten him to her dietary specifications. *Shall I climb in*, the Captain offered, *so you can stuff me with Wienerschnitzel and sausages, then eat me up?* I assured him that there were some better ways to torment and consume him. *Oh really?* The Captain whispered in my ear. His breath was warm. He nibbled on my lobe then gave it a playful bite.

We slipped into a group gathered outside the entrance to the Medieval Criminal Law Museum. The tour guide, a lanky American wearing a YALE Law sweatshirt, pointed to the cage and explained with a little Texas in his twang, *This here shame basket is something the Baker's Guild dreamed up. They didn't cotton to cheaters. Skimp on ingredients? Fall short of the weight requirements? You'd be the unhappy recipient of a baker's baptism. And my lord, it was better than a Baptist preacher on a Sunday. Plunged you right in the river. Or a pile of shit. Imagine,* he said, a wide grin spreading across the pimpled plain of his face. *Total immersion.*

He beckoned us to follow him. Along with the two gray-haired ladies from London, the young couple with a baby from Milwaukee, a Japanese family, and the backpackers from Halifax, Canadian flag patches prominently displayed on their packs. We shuffled into the house of horrors hosting a thousand years of crime and punishment, execution devices, and implements of torture used for extracting confessions. Like a game show host, the tour guide opened his arm offering the array: the manacles that looked like bear traps, throne-like chairs upholstered with spikes, thumbscrews, the rack. *It's just like Kafka y'all! Imagine the minds that dreamed this all up.*

He couldn't get enough of this stuff. That's why, he said, he'd deferred his admission to law school and his political ambitions to study, on a Fulbright, punishment design and criminal justice theory. Deterrence, rehabilitation, retribution, that sort of thing. The gig at the criminal law museum part of his fellowship.

The tour guide told us that before the collection was acquired by the museum, it had been curated for the private enjoyment of a nineteenth-century publisher and his wife. *Kept all this stuff in the basement of their castle hotel. They must have had some pretty kinky nights,* he said. When there was no response, he added, raising his eyebrows in quick suggestive arches, did he really have to spell it out? *C'mon now. Are you with me?* Nervous laughter rippled through the group. Moving on, the tour guide pointed out ancient texts prescribing taxes and death penalties. The detailed transcriptions of witch trials. The glass boxes displaying iron masks of shame; ones with snouts for men who acted like swine, ones with lolling tongues for blabbermouths. *There should be one with donkey ears for a tour guide who acts like an ass,* the Captain whispered.

The tour guide, his cowboy boots clopping to a country music song only he could hear, swaggered into a new wing. We followed him like baby ducks. *And now the pièce de résistance,* he said. *Ladies, a whole room devoted to you!*

The tour guide pointed out the most gruesome tortures, all of which were reserved for women. His favorites included the "breast ripper," the heated metal claw used to rip off the breast of a woman convicted of adultery. *I mean, who needs a scarlet letter when you've got one of these?*

And there was nothing so wonderfully diabolical as the beautifully crafted "pear of anguish," a pear-shaped device, with four sharp-edged petals, which blossomed with each turn of an ornately carved key, expanding into the orifice of the torturer's choice. For women, this cruel speculum was used to induce miscarriages and extract confessions of promiscuity.

I thought about the pears I stole from the orchard adjacent to my backyard in Ohio. How I used a melon baller to scoop the ripe pear flesh then baked it with brown sugar, cinnamon, and Quaker Oats for a perfect pear crumble. The time I stashed some in an old white cupboard in the garage, returning later to find them covered in ants. How, after that, just the mention of pears made my stomach churn. I thought about the boys back in Ohio and my fear that time my period refused to arrive. I imagined the cruel twist of the key and the sharp blades expanding inside of me.

The Captain grabbed my hand. *Let's get the hell of here*, he said.

The spell was broken. We motored out of the fairytale and into the future, with no bread crumbs to guide the way, me to the army base and the Captain to the border.

Upon his return, the Captain, his face tanned from his time in the field, taught me how to navigate a stick shift, so I could feel my own power. Then it was his turn to hold on as I careened the curves of the road at breakneck speeds. I drove us to Saltzburg for the Sound of Music Tour. To the abbey where the nuns wondered what to do about Maria. And then Mirabellplatz, to the Pegasus fountain where Julie Andrews and the Von Trapp children sang. In Berchtesgaden, we hiked up the mountain to Hitler's Eagle's Nest. We tried to reconcile the green, luscious beauty, the technicolor-blue skies and the dazzling snow-capped peaks with all the evil people who once gathered there.

That night we stayed in a little pension. I was ravenous for the Captain, so we skipped dinner. This time I climbed on top. Leaned into his earthy soldier smell, licked his salty neck, guided his calloused hands. He growled with approval when I told him what I wanted, demanded his compliance.

At the end of the summer, the Captain took me to the airport. When I cried and told him I didn't want to leave, he assured me that it was the adventure, not him, I would miss. That I was not the same person I had been three months before. *It's a pity you have to grow up,* he said tucking my hair behind my ears then kissing the top of my head. *But I like the idea of you out there in the world, turning heads, busting balls.*

Back in Ohio, memories of the Captain stitched themselves into my DNA. I disbanded the honeycomb of boys and finished law school, studied for the bar exam, secured a job. I took up golf, and bourbon and cigars and men.

Years would go by without the slightest thought of that summer and then a walk in the woods, the smell of pine needles, a waft of bratwurst grilling on a backyard barbecue, the mélange of salt and pepper, coriander, nutmeg, and marjoram, the promise of hearty German mustard and a crusty roll would whisper into my ear.

And then, like last night, the Captain would slip into my dreams, a phantom of pleasure for sure but also a niggling feeling, a jab at my conscience that I had left something undone.

The man beside me snores lightly into the pillows, oblivious to my indiscretions while we slumbered. I nudge him awake with my foot, my toes sinking into his middle-aged belly. I tell him he should stay in bed while I get ready, let himself out once I leave for work. I tell him I'll give him a call. Assure him we can meet up again soon.

Out of habit, I turn on the news. It follows me throughout my day, on the TV, the radio, on any number of my electronic devices, from my bedroom to the kitchen as I smash avocado and a pinch red pepper flakes onto my toast, as I drive to Starbucks for my vanilla iced latte with oat milk then downtown, as I ride the elevator up thirty-three floors to my office, the nicest one a dying rust belt city can fashion. My framed diplomas and gold-sealed certificates from the Supreme Court of Ohio brag on the walls. I draft contracts and facilitate deals, leaving the less lucrative job of pursuing justice to those who claim they don't care about the money.

An alert flashes up on my computer. I click the video link. It's the same Texas congressman who's been trending on all the social platforms for the last few weeks, the networks scrambling to cover the latest sensation gone viral. The media package shows his campaign slogan plastered on billboards in Lubbock and Waco and Wichita Falls then segues into clips from SNL lampooning him, reimagining those same billboards with a new slogan "Make the Middle Ages Great Again." The Texan eager to extend his influence beyond the state's borders, formally announces his bid for U.S. Senate, hinting that he may even run for president someday. In the interview, he touts his crime initiative, especially the bill he co-sponsored, and signed into law by the governor: SB 476 authorizing the use of the Pearculum™ confession extraction device. No training, license, or registration required. *The device* he says *pairs nicely with the Texas Bounty Law which grants a tidy sum to anyone who ferrets out accomplices assisting with the unnatural disruption of a woman's reproduction cycle.*

I lean in for a closer look, enlarge the image on my screen. Could it be the tour guide? Tall and lanky like a scarecrow, a grin spreads across his pocked marked face, he raises his eyebrows twice in quick succession as he introduces his wife, the dazzling brunette by his side.

Without intervention, it will only be a matter of time before the use of the Pearculum™ will spread like a fungus, hopscotch from state to state. The *New York Times* will launch an investigative series, win a Pulitzer for profiling women with mangled wombs, no longer able to conceive or carry a wanted child to term given the unforgiving manipulation of the confessional device. The parade of horribles will be endless.

I admit, it doesn't sink in right away. What I need to do next. I stare into my palms, conjure a handful of foreign coins. I remember the sausage stand, my hunger. I wonder how much it will cost me. How many confessions I will need to make along the way. I feel the scrape of the melon baller, the twist of the key. I remember the grip of the steering wheel, the hard shaft of the stick in my hand, the power in taking the road, shifting gears. I know I can no longer afford the privilege of looking the other way.

Mack the Knife

THE PARTNERS HAVE BEEN TALKING. This is what they do at the end of the summer. Decide your fate. They decide whether you will return to school—the last year of law school—the last year of twenty years of school—empty-handed or clutching a golden ticket: an offer of employment, with benefits you don't understand, a stipend for the following summer while you study for the bar, enough to quit the waitressing job and still pay your rent, enough to pay for Guinness that you will drink with the guys at The Flats even though it tastes like the dregs from yesterday's coffee pot, and enough to buy groceries, something other than jam sandwiches, something with meat.

They discuss your credentials in the Main Boardroom, the one with the twenty-four-foot-long conference table, its sturdy legs made of black mahogany, its top made of cherry with a Bolivian rosewood inlay. Thirty Chippendale chairs to be occupied by twenty-nine men and one woman. The feet on the table and chairs are classic brass claw and ball. Everything is provincial, old money, hunter green punctuated with red piping. Pictures of pheasants and horns, hounds, and horses adorn the short walls. On the long walls, portraits of dead partners stare down with jowled frowns.

In the boardroom they politely discuss your research and writing skills, the way your words flow persuasively, your typos, your ubiquitous misspelling of ubiquitous. They discuss your professional appearance, your clothes, your hair, your cheerleader smile, your inability to present a brief without a question mark in your delivery. Like a child looking for approval. Like a student asking a teacher for an A.

Over lunch they talk about your double-breasted, oversized suits. The skirts that hang too long, except that one navy blue dress you wore with the black patent pumps, the one that made them forget your skinny ankles, your chicken legs.

Over dinner they talk about that time they saw you running the city streets. They'll remark that underneath the layers of wool and polyester and beige-colored nylons, you have muscular legs that could crush a man's head, that you are otherwise surprisingly small with smooth, tan skin and freckled shoulders.

Over a cigar and brandy they talk about your hidden places, the mystery of you. And yet: Wallenda never talks this way. He's too busy, too married to his work and his wife and his rat pack of kids named after mountain ranges: Sierra, Rocky, Andes, Laurel, Darby, and Plume.

Bennett never talks this way; he says you look like a child.

Hillcrest never talks this way; he says you look like somebody's teenaged daughter.

DeLuca never talks this way because he savors his preoccupation with you. Because you are neither woman nor child. You are feral, a bedraggled cat, untamed yet malleable in some indiscernible way. He sees unlimited potential to mold you into something wicked, something delightful, something mean. You know this because DeLuca tells you. The night he asks you to stay late, past the mandatory summer associate departure time. He hands you twelve inches of environmental regulations with some acronym you can no longer remember, printed on paper as thin as tissue. He recites the pertinent facts, then poses a query and because time is of the essence, he asks you to provide the answer later that evening, after his meeting with the client.

You struggle over emergency responses and hazardous substances, inactive waste disposal sites, potentially responsible persons and Superfund sites. There are five-year cleanup plans and your mind wanders to your college honors thesis, to Soviet Russia, the proletariat and Stalin's Five Year Plans. You are thinking rapid industrialization and the slaughter of thousands of farm animals. And then you're thinking about *Dr. Zhivago*, six hundred pages of starvation, longing, and loneliness: Yuri with Tonya but Yuri desperate for Lara.

It's eight thirty and, from your office window, you can see the setting sun cast pinkish-gray shadows onto the muddy waters of the Maumee River. For a minute you could be anywhere—somewhere exotic with rivers and bridges, Paris or Venice or Amsterdam or St. Petersburg. You do not hear DeLuca come in. He is behind you, watching you watch the tugboats dragging flats of coal. He smells like a man, like Scotch and tobacco; like leather, like an oiled saddle or Jimmer's baseball mitt. He smells like shaving cream and ballpoint pen. He smells like history.

He spins you around and you take in his yellow silk tie, his white pinpoint cotton collar, the tie bar, the monogrammed shirt pocket and the gold cuff links as he reaches for the back of your ponytail. With one swift tug, he breaks the rubber band corralling your hair. Like a rumor, it spills out onto your shoulders and beyond, slow then fast, down to the middle of your back.

His fingers rake through the tangles. The mess grows with his ministrations. He asks you why you never wear it down.

You respond that it is too wild and too big for your face.

Like your clothes, he says. Who can tell what you are underneath it all?

His fingers grip and claw, gather your tresses, wind them into a fistful of you. He gently tugs then yanks you closer. He smells your hair, breathes in your essence. His lips whisper against your temple, your eyelid, your ear lobe, your neck. You forget the wife you met at the firm picnic a few weeks back. The wife sporting a hot pink polo and pearls, with her homemade peach cobbler and her pale pink children who resembled fat little pigs. You push down the thoughts of another wife you know, your own mother for fuck's sake, a trembling cigarette slanting sideways from her mouth, ashes ready to tumble. You ignore the memory of the day she found the secret checking account, the scent of another woman in her husband's pockets, his shoes, his socks. You refuse the image of you and Jimmer and Margot being told to pack the station wagon, the day she told you it would be better for everyone if the four of you simply got in the car and drove off a cliff. You forget because at this moment you are powerful, you, the creator of desire. You can feel it pressing hard against you. DeLuca's lips linger on your clavicle, the left side, the one you broke riding your ten-speed down Ridgewood Road on your way home from band camp. Like the rest of you, it never healed quite right. He nuzzles the spot where the bone knitted together into a knot. You slide your hand inside his coat, you feel the cascade of his middle-aged flesh underneath the starch. He feels used, secondhand and old. Oh god you remember, oh God. You try to pull away except now he is no longer whispering his affection.

I can't get enough of you, he whimpers. He is tugging at your pantyhose, fumbling with his zipper. He's straddling your lap, the oppressive weight of him on your thighs, pulling your hair and thrusting and you are protesting to the monogrammed pocket on his chest and trying to push him away.

A sound in the hallway, the bell of the elevator door opening, the closing of file cabinets. You hear Bennett strolling the hallways singing "Mack the Knife."

DeLuca withdraws himself, releases your hair, adjusts his trousers. Just like that, he's gone.

It's dark. The lights on the bridges twinkle and sneer. Your reflection watches you pull up your pantyhose, which now have a run. Your reflection knows who you are, what you have become. You hurt in places even DeLuca can't penetrate.

Despite your lack of confidence, your inability to spell, your spinster looks and chicken legs, you get an offer. You take the letter, printed on the firm's letterhead, into your office, the one that will belong to next year's summer associate. You close the door and grab the black-handled scissors you never used all summer. While you watch the tugboats drag coal to Port Huron, you cut your hair.

Devil's Hole Road

DUST AND POLLEN FLOATED IN from the fields just beyond the town's solitary block of businesses, the diner, the dressmaker, the bank. Everything weary, parched from the heat and lack of rain, sweatered in a yellowish-green patina that stung my eyes and lumped my throat. Even the courthouse clock tower yawned, exhausted as its hands ticked through the thick, panting air. Dalton had left me stranded in the parking lot, clutching my briefcase and the judge's order to get the hell out of his courtroom.

"No use looking for him. He's already gone," Liza Abbott said. My patent leather heels sank into the gooey blacktop as she climbed into her snub-nosed pickup truck. Rust dappled its bricky hood and fenders. "Might as well come with me."

"I don't suppose you've got cabs out here?" I said.

"Nope. And even if we did—they wouldn't drive you to the farm. It's too far out."

The hinge creaked as I opened the door. It was late August. The weatherman had said to expect record heat, possibly in the three-digits, pop-up showers, maybe even a tornado. Sweat pooled at the waistband of my hose, then trickled down my panties. More sweat collected at the back of my knees. It seemed like ages since the morning when Mad Dog shoved a new case file in my hands and announced that it was to time rip off the training wheels. If I could muster up the courage, I was going to kill him when I got back to the city.

Liza had already pulled off her Keds and her white ankle socks. Underneath her shapeless farmhouse calico, she was shimmying up a pair of cut-off jean shorts, hips lifted as she zipped and buttoned. She pulled the dress off over her head. For a moment she was topless. I looked away as she slipped on a white tank top. When I looked back, she was taking the pins out of her hair, releasing a wave of black curls, which she fluffed into a messy nest. She looked over at me, all buttoned up in my gray suit, and said, "You're gonna suffocate in that get-up, you know."

Earlier, when Liza was sitting on the witness stand, she told the judge she hadn't planned on buying new windows the day Dalton showed up in his long white Cadillac complaining of car trouble and wanting to use the phone. Liza had been reluctant to accommodate the man, but then Mama came out of the kitchen, sized up the handsome stranger on the other side of the screen door, appreciated his pleated khaki trousers, his crisp white button-down, cuffs rolled up two turns, admired his forearms, boyishly freckled but manly in the wrist, and said they might as well invite him in.

Liza's brown-suited attorney, Mr. Dalrymple, coaxed the story from her. She had been timid on the witness stand, first tugging on her big lacy collar, then twirling a coil of hair that had escaped her schoolmarm bun. She recited with a bit of a twang how Mama had taken a liking to the man, offered him a limeade, took him on a tour of the house. Dalton examined all the windows, asked if they were original, did they open, let in cold air. He pointed out a few cracks, a broken sash, a bullet hole. "It was obscene the way he caressed them windows," Liza said, first speaking to the judge and then directing her gaze towards Dalton. "Almost like he'd dipped his fingertips in honey, like he was stroking a lady."

The judge coughed, looked over at me, and inquired as to whether I'd like to object, but I had nothing. I'd been hypnotized by Liza's flawless skin, wondering if she had a string of rock candy hidden deep within her *Little House on the Prairie* pockets.

Dalton slumped in his chair, drummed his fingers, his fake Rolex bragging with a rhythmic click against the scarred plaintiff's table, until the judge hollered at him to cut that shit out and ordered the bailiff to turn on the big fan. The judge advised Liza to speak louder for the remainder of her testimony.

"That's when the plaintiff told Mama that he was in the window business. The next thing you know he's got out his tape measure and we're signing papers. Never did make his phone call. After Mama handed him a check made out to Galaxy Windows Inc. for the down payment, he closed the hood of his car and just drove away. I told Mama that I was worried, that something just wasn't right, but she said she was investing in my future."

"Did you ever get your windows?" asked Mr. Dalrymple.

"Yes. A crew of men showed up one day. Spent hours. But Dalton never came back. Not that I'm aware of. Even in the winter when the windows iced up and got all foggy. Some of them didn't fit at all. Mama was kind of disappointed about that."

The judge sighed. Looked at his watch, then zeroed in on Dalton. "You ever go check on those windows?"

"No, sir." Dalton stared at the table, shifted in his chair, glanced at Liza. "See, the windows were already made and they were manu-factured according to that house's specifications. Special order, you know? We couldn't use them on a different job."

To me, Dalton whispered, "Aren't you supposed to be saying something smart right about now?"

A dark look crossed the judge's face. "So you never inspected the windows, after they were installed?"

"Nope." Dalton leaned back in his chair, pushed his wavy ginger hair away from his forehead. And with that, the judge ordered every-one out of the courtroom until the windows were looked at. I had rid-den in from Toledo with Dalton to facilitate my first and only review of the file, but he sped away without me, hollering through the ex-haust and the thumping stereo base that he'd meet me there. Left me with my heels digging asphalt, my confidence swooning in the heat.

The Abbott place was in the next county over, forty-something miles away.

"You're gonna have to roll down the window. Henry here," Liza said, patting the dashboard, "didn't come with air conditioning. And take off that jacket and pantyhose for god's sake. It must be at least ninety-something degrees out. It's gonna take a while to get there."

As she pulled out, Liza turned on the AM radio. It mostly crackled and buzzed. Just a thin ribbon of music audible over Henry's muffler and the static. Liza fiddled with the tuner.

"Must be a storm coming. Can never get a station when the weather turns."

She clicked off what sounded like INXS, pushed in the lighter, pulled out a pack of cigarettes. She offered me one before she lit hers, took a deep long drag, and blew smoke out the window. Wind whipped her hair. Perspiration collected in the sweet little hollow of her neck. Her tank top clung to her damp skin, and I stared at her erect nipples pressing against the thin cloth, plummy silver dollar-sized areola, the curve of her breast.

Liza looked over at me still buttoned, encased in nylon and cotton and wool. She shook her head. "You shouldn't be such a prude."

Heat rose up from the pavement, wavy shimmers of curvy glass. We stopped at a Marathon station to get gas. It was an old-timey place. A lanky guy in overalls sauntered over to pump, took one look at Liza and started making plans to meet at Jukes on Friday night. He fetched us two bottles of orange pop and patted the side of the car before we drove away, shouting, "Better hurry up and get home. A storm's coming."

"That's what I hear," she said, laughing.

Underneath a thin veil of hazy clouds, the sky blushed crystal blue.

Soon the roads got dustier, surrounded by a straight, flat checkerboard of corn and soybean and rich green squares of alfalfa dotted with purple blooms. White farmhouses and grain bins and silos, red barns with Mail Pouch ads painted on the side. Deep trenches ridged either side of the highway. Cattails and jewelweed sprang from the trenches. We rumbled by patches of orange ditch-bank lilies. It felt good, the hot wind on my face, to watch the racing pavement. I rubbed the back of my neck, my fingers remembering hair that was no longer there.

Liza shouted over the din of the truck's muffler, "That your first trial?"

The matter before the Judge was a hearing, not a trial, so technically I wasn't lying when I said, "No. Not my first." I wasn't about to explain why I was the one sitting at the table instead of someone more senior, how, even blindsided, it was better than being sequestered in the law library writing briefs or fetching cups of coffee.

"Why'd you want to become a lawyer anyway?" she said.

I shrugged. Visions of lonely Saturday afternoons, black and white movies offered up on one of three channels, Hepburn and Tracey in *Adam's Rib*, husband and wife lawyers, he a prosecutor, she a defense attorney. All that smart banter, dinner parties, she in her black evening gown, her elegant clavicles, the swan of her neck, the ribbon of spine as Tracey zipped her up. "I was a kid when I decided. I thought it would make me feel important. Not so invisible," I said.

"Did it work?"

I didn't answer. Just looked out the window.

After a while, I angled out of my suit jacket, rolled up my sleeves, and undid a few of the top buttons of my blouse. I kicked off my shoes and before long was shimmying out my pantyhose and rolling my skirt up to my thighs. I pulled my blouse from the stiff confines of my cinched waistband and released the bottom three buttons. For a moment, I considered stripping down to my camisole.

Liza tried the radio again. "Feel better?"

At that moment, with the dull summer heat furnacing about me, the wind in my face, Duran Duran singing "Hungry Like a Wolf," Liza's hair whipping like a black funnel cloud, I knew I would always feel better riding in the truck with Liza.

Finally, we turned left onto a dirt road, a skunk stripe of greenish-brown grass running down the middle. We bounced, wobbled over a rock or two, and stopped in front of an old farmhouse with a covered front porch. Most of the white paint had peeled off, revealing a ghostly gray underneath, something like prairie driftwood.

"Well. Here we are." She reached under the seat for a pair of short white boots.

"Welcome to the Great Black Swamp."

I looked at the endless flat landscape, treeless except for a single magnificent weeping willow out back. I thought swamp meant the

Everglades, murky water, algae, mosquitos, alligators, foliage, somber trees searching for light. Not farmland. Not Ohio.

I was tucking in my blouse, slipping back into my black patent leathers when Liza came around the back of the truck, looped her arm through mine and hollered.

"Mama, I brought the lawyer out to see the windows."

Mama emerged from the house, the screen door clacking shut behind her. She had long, thick, gray hair with wavy flourishes of white that curled at her temples. She wore frayed bell-bottom blue jeans, clogs, and a white peasant blouse. I had been picturing a matronly woman with a gingham house dress and white apron, not a glamorous middle-aged hippie. She skipped down the front porch steps.

"Welcome, lawyer!" she said, hugging me like I was a long-lost friend. I wondered if she knew that I was the enemy, for the other side, possibly the wrong side.

She hugged Liza as well.

"I didn't know you'd be bringing a *lady* lawyer. She's precious, bless her heart," Mama said smiling at me. "Big day in the city?"

"Yeah, if you call Wauseon a city," said Liza.

"That old worthless hound dog lawyer of ours bail on us?"

"Yep."

"And the Galaxy Window Boy?"

"Not coming."

They both had a good laugh about that. But suddenly I wondered what the joke was. Not coming? What did she mean they're not coming? How was I going to get home?

"Not to worry, dear. Liza will drive you home as soon as you take a look at the windows," Mama said. "And I'm not a mind reader. You wouldn't do well in a poker game, I'm afraid. I'd stick with the truth if I were you."

I followed the pair up the rickety steps onto the porch and into the house. I'd expected to be greeted with a velvet settee, wingback chairs, side tables covered in lace doilies and porcelain knick-knacks. Instead, the house was littered with buckets of dirt, boxes of rocks, piles of clay, a potter's wheel. Clay figurines of the human and animal variety posed on dented metal erector shelves. Large canvases, with their backs turned, lined the walls; tubes of oil pigment, brushes, and a blank canvas set up on an easel. An oak bookcase housed mason jars, watery prisons filled with curls of bark, lemon grass, allspice berries, cardamom pods, and lavender buds. I held one up to the light, shook it. Sugar snowed then sank to the bottom.

"Tonic syrup," Mama offered. "Ancient recipe. Cures all sorts of aches and pains, fevers and what-not. Those jars have to steep a few more days."

Mama insisted on stirring up some fresh limeade so I could give it a try. Liza slipped out the back door, grabbed a bottle of homemade tonic water from the cellar, and pinched a handful of wild mint growing next to the back stoop.

Meanwhile, I examined the first-floor windows. My fingers trailed the windowsills, the rotten wood, the bullet hole. I unlatched the locks, pushed a window open that banged shut the minute I left it. Mama laughed when she heard the crash. She emerged from the kitchen, "Those aren't the new ones, honey," she said. Mama handed me a tall frosted glass.

The room darkened as if it were night and just like that a torrent of rain thudded, pounding the roof, and a gust of wind ushered in the smell of earth, dank and rich with decay before slamming the front door shut. I sipped my limeade, both tart and bitter. Mama turned on a lamp, and I could see my reflection in the window, hawkish features hidden in the swell of a little girl face. It was distorted, wavy in the pock-marked glass, the bullet hole piercing my breastbone on the left side. I felt a brief electric twitch in my heart. I took another sip. It tasted like childhood. It tasted like climbing forbidden trees, like the day I fell and got the wind knocked out of me, unable to breathe and no words to speak. Splinters. It tasted like the day I didn't make the cheerleading team. Waiting 'til midnight for the phone call that never came. Like the time that man slid his fingers into places they didn't belong. In the window, I saw empty vessels, sorrow, regret. All swirling with the storm outside.

I could feel Mama and Liza hovering behind me, as if watching the unveiling of my soul.

"That's enough, Mama," said Liza.

"Indeed," Mama said, clicking off the light.

The rain crescendoed into a thunderous applause, faded to a hazy mist, then stopped. I shook my head. I was dazed.

Mama ushered me outside. Steam rose from the earth. A lightning bolt zagged in the distance where it was still dark as night, still pouring. A clap of thunder. The sun blinked on. It was hotter than ever. Hotter than any day I could remember.

We sat on the swing, Liza next to me gently pushing us back and forth with her white-booted foot. Our perch was rickety: it moaned and creaked as we swayed. Her arm rested on the back of the swing. She tugged at the sleeve of my blouse. "People don't like coming out here on account of the name."

"It's true," Mama said. "There used to be a sign at the crossroads with the name of our road, but the college kids from Bowling Green kept stealing it. For room décor. Then one day a frat boy disappeared. His fraternity brothers thought he was playing a prank because of the legend that this area was sort of like the Bermuda Triangle—back in the day with the swamp. The mud in some places came up to a horse's belly. The trees? So thick you couldn't see daylight. Settlers, soldiers went in and never made their way out. Swallowed up like quicksand, sucked them right into hell, some people say. Anyway, after a day or two, the fraternity brothers got scared and went to the police. Hundreds of volunteers searched for days, made a mess stomping through the cornfields. The only thing they found was a red-laced boot and the road sign stuck in an old bog, one of the last remnants of the swamp. Now, we're just State Route 61. But everyone who's been around these parts for a while knows that this property resides on Devil's Hole Road. That squirrelly Galaxy fellow is too damn scared to come here. Imagine that? A grown man on a sunny summer afternoon. And leaving you to fend for yourself. Sure wasn't scared when he had windows to sell."

Mama, it turned out, was a geologist. She was fascinated by the invisible landscape, everything that lies underneath. Bought the old farmhouse so that she could study the earth, the soil and its ecosystem. I learned Liza wasn't her daughter. Mama had found her squatting in the house, painting huge canvasses of wildflowers and cattails and willows and dark things. Instead of kicking her out, Mama asked her to stay. They had some arrangement but didn't offer to share the details.

We continued rocking back and forth. By then, I had kicked off my pumps again. My bare toes traced the splintered paint under my feet. My big toe worked to dislodge a gray triangle. Liza scooted closer, her nearness startling. I felt a current, an unmistakable yet unnamable static in the air. Goosebumps prickled my arms. I was breathless, from the heat I supposed.

Mama sat in one of two rocking chairs. Her hair pushed back off her forehead with a pair of reading glasses revealing a widow's peak. A dark mole dotted the corner of one cheek. She stared at me with her midnight-blue eyes.

Everything slowed, time stood still on account of the heat as if we were sitting on a veranda at the beginning a sultry Southern play. Nothing urgent. My heart rate slowed. In this moment, there were no clients, no billable hours, no stacks of briefs and case books, nothing to be filed. No angry judges. I gave in, released myself to the moment. I once again unbuttoned my blouse but this time I took it off, rolled up my skirt like a Catholic school girl. A random breeze nibbled at my skin. I held my icy glass dripping with condensation against my forehead.

"Twenty thousand years ago, this whole area was covered by glaciers," Mama said. She nodded outward past the porch toward the barn, the fields, the silos, the deserted country highway. "Imagine that. Everything you see out there. Covered in ice, one mile thick. Seventeen and a half football fields deep." She paused so I could visualize the immensity. "It all came from the North."

"Trouble always comes from up north," said Liza. "Hockey players, lumberjacks, Mounties." Liza touched her fingers to her mouth hiding a memory, the bloom of a smile.

"The climate changed. Canada grew frigid cold. Winter arrived and, like a bad house guest, never left, for thousands of years, dumping its massive suitcases full of ice and snow," Mama continued.

I thought of *The Lion, The Witch and The Wardrobe*. Like Narnia. Always winter but never Christmas.

"So much of it piled up and accumulated that a great ice sheet squeezed out from under the mound and pushed outward due to its own weight. Imagine a giant rolling pin and a lump of dough, working the lump back and forth spreading it until the dough and everything under it is as flat as pie crust. But this glacier, it ground like a pickaxe over exposed rocks and mountains. The icy fist of nature pulverizing everything in its wake. It gouged and scraped the landscape, depositing sand, silt, gravel, and clay."

"Don't forget the sea creatures," said Liza. She kicked off her boots, pulled her hair off the nape of her neck, and scooted even closer.

"And sea creatures, crushed calcified bones of sea creatures," Mama said.

I looked out past the front porch, across the street and the cornfields beyond. I tried to imagine great mounds of prehistoric squid and eel. Ancient mermaids.

"The last ice age ended ten thousand years ago. Once the ice began to melt, great torrents of water gushed, searching for an outlet to the sea. In this area, the glacier gouged out an ancient lake, Lake Maumee, which was lined with an impermeable blue clay bottom. The lake grew and shrank over the centuries, a slow-moving, throbbing force of nature."

Liza plucked an ice cube from my glass, sucked on it and then rolled it on the hollow of her neck, her hairline, her cleavage. I stared into my limeade—bits of light green pulp had floated to the top.

"When the water finally receded, it left behind the swamp," Mama said. "Black mucky waters, vipers, plagues of mosquitos, malaria."

"And swamp creatures," added Liza. "Made of clay."

A car rumbled up the driveway, wheels spinning in the dirt and gravel crunching. The judge emerged from the car in a cloud of dust. I hastily grabbed my blouse, threw it on over my camisole, tucking it in. I grabbed my shoes. Mama stood up.

"Hello, Lilith," the Judge said.

"Judge. What brings you here? It's been ages, after all. You come for some tonic?"

"I got a call from the Galaxy boy saying he couldn't make it. Some sort of medical emergency. Thought I'd come out and take a look at the windows myself. And collect Ms. Armstrong. There's a tornado warning."

"Come on in, Judge." Mama handed him her untouched glass of limeade. "You may as well have a drink while you're here. It's good for your ague."

"Thank you, ma'am. It is about time for my afternoon shakes."

"The windows in question are upstairs."

Liza and I watched the two retreat into the house. We heard footsteps as they walked to the second floor. Soon it seemed the entire house was rattling. Back and forth, back and forth with an occasional bang against a wall.

"Let's get out of here," Liza said. She jumped off the swing mid-rock, and limeade splashed onto the webby vee connecting my fingers and thumb. Liza watched me as I licked it off. I hesitated, looked up at the second-floor windows.

"Come on," Liza said, grabbing my sticky hand. "They'll be awhile." And just like that, Liza and I were holding hands, strolling to the gray barn just beyond the house.

I was hoping for horses, or pigs, or squawking chickens, but it didn't look like that type of farm. Then I imagined hay bales and shovels and rakes, a rusted tractor to match Liza's truck. Liza unlatched the barn door, and with a dramatic tug she slid the door to the right. I gasped. The barn was filled with windows. New, old, ancient. Every shape and size. Hundreds, stacked and filed every which way.

Liza laughed. "Mama has a thing for windows."

I waded through the tangle of frames.

Each window was tagged, inventoried with a date, a place, and a name. One read: "Private John Stryker, Western Reserve Road, 1812," another: "Abraham Tanner, Perrysburg, 1937." Another: "Bog Boy, BGSU, 1984."

"Are the Galaxy windows here? The ones that didn't fit?"

Liza pointed to the corner in the back.

The Galaxy windows were wrapped in white paper, one tagged nonetheless. A flourish of calligraphy gleamed wet with ink. I looked to Liza for an explanation, but she had turned away from me. The delicate wings of her shoulder blades trembled as she stared beyond the barn doors, into the fields, where swampy things once lived.

THE GIRL WAS A WILD LITTLE THING, slight with tangled hair, ragged fingernails, and impossibly dirty feet. Pretty doesn't come to mind but I found her mouth beguiling, its sap-stained corners, the dusting of blue-black soil sprinkled like cookie crumbs on her lips. I told my brother's wife about her, how the girl wedged high up in an oak tree had pelted me with green acorns that summer I ran the trail at Swann Creek Park. Each loop was only about a mile or so, and I had made up my mind to do six or seven laps before I punched the clock for my shift at the Dairy Mart. As far as my brother was concerned, running was my only talent, my only ticket to college, the only way he and his wife could be released from the burden of me. I generally agreed with his assessment. I had an unforgiveable, lackadaisical nature and a deep aversion to schoolwork. But I could run with abandon. I reveled the burn in my chest and the rhythmic thwap of my Adidas pounding mile after mile.

Otherwise, I was a slacker. I stayed up late watching Johnny Carson on the black and white portable, sipping gin any which way (up, on the rocks, or dirty with olive juice and a splash of vermouth) and once the TV had forsaken me and all the networks signed off for the night, I reached for one of my mother's books, of which there were hundreds, and another shot or two of gin. In this way, I puzzled together my mother in a way that I couldn't puzzle math or my brother or our father.

My brother's wife convinced him to accept what she called my eccentricities brought on by what she believed to be persistent and delayed grief. So he didn't say a word when he found me lounging in a bubble bath reading a swollen copy of Ayn Rand or lying down in the back seat of my mother's car, the one that hadn't crashed, with *Silent Spring*. But the day my brother came down to breakfast and found me sporting our father's fishing hat, fishing lures and flies jiggling as I wolfed down the last of the Cap'n Crunch, thumbing through a dog-eared and underlined copy of Jacqueline Susann's *The Love Machine*? Now that was something else.

"What the fuck are you reading, Rusty?" he said. He smacked it out of my hand and proceeded to pound me with his law school hornbooks. Those things were thick and heavy hardcover treatises, nothing like my mother's paperbacks. He heaved *Corbin on Contracts*, *Prosser on Torts*, *Laurence Tribe on Con Law*. Even *Black's Law Dictionary* had a turn. They left welts and later bruises.

I told my brother's wife how I was just hitting my stride at the trail, soon to be in the zone, where a euphoria better than a boozy haze could be found, where I'd soon be floating rather than racing to the top of the hill—when the first round of insults hit my shoulders, making contact with the bruised places my brother's justice had administered. "Hey!" I shouted. I picked up a rock, intending to throw it the next time around. It felt good and jagged, authoritative in my fist. But the next time around I heard laughter; there was no menace in it, just delight. I looked up, salty sweat stinging my eyes, the sun filtered through the leaves obscuring my vision. I looked higher still and saw her, a girl around my age straddling a branch, bare feet swinging, the folds of her white dress aflutter. Instantly, I was bewitched.

I wanted to show off—I ran fast—gathered tokens along the trail and left them at the base of the tree with each passing loop. The jagged rock, a fistful of Queen Anne's lace and wild snapdragons, a handful of mushrooms, fiddleheads, a salamander. I sang her a song. I pleaded with her to spare my heart. Wouldn't she please come down?

And yet, she refused.

I hadn't planned to hit her, or hurt her. I just—wanted her. The rotten core of me picked up the rock that I had offered earlier as tribute and hurled it, heard it ricochet off the trunk with a smack. On the final loop, as I crested the hill, I saw a body. It was the girl lying flat on her back, dress askew—exposing one small breast and a hint of her private regions, the proper names for which didn't readily come to mind. My brain could only summon paperback euphemisms and back-of-the-school-bus vulgarities we boys snickered loudly and often. Her glassy green eyes stared up into the sky.

Certain I had killed her, too dumb to check her pulse or try CPR, I prepared her body for the inevitable. I wept as I arranged her limbs. I plucked leaves and twigs from her dress. Before I covered the porcelain swell of her chest, I extracted a splinter and kissed the angry spot where it had been lodged. I raked my fingers through her auburn hair but it refused to be tamed, it seemed rooted somehow—so I braided a crown with flowers and fiddleheads and wreathed them into a halo on her head. I thought I should say a prayer or something, but since I didn't believe in God anymore, I conjured a poem from one of my mother's books, the one about Xanadu and Kubla Khan:

In Xanadu did Kubla Khan
A stately pleasure-dome decree:
Where Alph, the sacred river, ran
Through caverns measureless to man
Down to a sunless sea.

The dead girl smiled so I lingered. Marveled at the beauty of death because—even in this pretend version—it was lovely and more than I had previously been permitted to see.

I bowed my head and whispered, "Who are you?"

The tree quivered, its limbs sighing with a ribbon of summer breeze. A warbler trilled to the far-off percussion of a woodpecker's rapid-fire drill. And then she wrapped her legs around my waist, pulled me toward her, flipped us around, her on top, straddling me. She pinned my arms above my head, leaned in and kissed me, hard then softly, with her dirty mouth. She smelled like juniper and honeysuckle, tasted like spiders and loamy earth. When she finally told me her name, she spoke like a fairy story, sentences riddled in rhyme.

"The trees call me Phoebe," she said. Her voice mossy, a thick slurry of twigs and bitter berries. A little bird with a lavender tongue. Her pelvis a hot insistent pressure. "I am the guardian of this grove. With the power vested in me," she said, the full weight of her pressing harder, "I claim you as my consort." Then she promised she'd share with me the secrets of the universe, what cannot be said in words, all that she had learned from talking to the trees.

I returned to the shade of the great oak every morning that summer. Sometimes, I'd linger for hours hoping to catch a glimpse of her. Sometimes, she'd be waiting for me with a wood nymph's smile.

After high school graduation. My brother's wife couldn't convince my brother to indulge my intention to major in poetry or philosophy.

"I mean, what kind of bullshit is that, Rusty?" he said.

So I majored in journalism and landed a job with the Toledo Blade. It was a print and pay situation. Ten cents a word. Given my lack of enthusiasm for the kind of assignments awarded to young reporters (The Peach Section—weddings, funerals, movie reviews, Peach Girl profiles), it wasn't long before I was evicted from my shitty apartment. I slept in my car for a few weeks before I summoned the courage to ask my brother and his wife if I could return to the fold and crash on their couch. He was working at the law firm by then, hoping to become the youngest partner. She had quit her job to concentrate on baby-making. My brother had responded tenderly the first time (even the second and third time) when she confessed that the life inside her had inexplicably expired. From the sidelines, I watched him cradle her, bring her cups of tea, rub her feet.

But the fourth time, four months in, on the cusp of the big trial, the night before *voir dire*, she interrupted a meeting with the jury consultant. The news about her incompetent cervix was not received with great compassion. I took her to the clinic, held her hand (despite the doctor's outraged and ardent objections) while he scraped and suctioned the residual fetal tissue from her womb, while my brother and the jury consultant discussed peremptory challenges and the vulnerabilities of the jury pool.

The procedure didn't take very long. Afterwards, I drove my brother's wife home, stopping on the way to buy her sanitary pads and Tylenol at the convenience store. I also bought us a video, potato chips and French onion dip, Heavenly Hash ice cream and cheap red wine.

I settled her on the sofa with the snacks, wrapped her in an old afghan, and popped *The Princess Bride* into the VCR. The machine zip, zip, zipped and whined. The screen turned black. I pushed the eject button, releasing the case and loops of videotape tethered to an invisible hand deep inside. I grabbed her spoon, licked off the marshmallowy chocolate, lifted the little door, peered inside the dark chamber and was about to insert the spoon into the VCR's womb when my brother's wife yelled, "Stop!"

I thanked her for saving me from certain electrical shock and reached over to pull the plug. But she confessed as she grabbed the spoon back and plunged it into the ice cream tub that she wasn't saving me. The mangle of tape was just too much for her to bear.

We sat there for a long time—passing the tub and the spoon back and forth. Refilling our glasses. Staring at the speechless TV, divining meaning in its silence. When we ran out of wine, I went in search of gin. I found a couple of airplane minis stashed behind a battered and yellowed copy of *The Little Prince* from which I read out loud to her well into the night.

I showed her the illustrations as if I were a kindergarten teacher at story hour. She laughed at the pictures of the snake and the hat and the elephant and the little prince with his yellow scarf flagging. Noted how lucky he was, that prince, to own a rose and three volcanoes. But she soon fell sullen and teary-eyed, turned her face away, her chest heaving. She unscrewed the tiny bottle of Tanqueray and downed it with three determined gulps. "He shouldn't have left the rose there—all by herself—on that asteroid." Flicking the tears away, she repositioned herself on the sofa, stretching her legs and settling her feet into my lap. I watched her fingertips trace the circumference of her empty belly in slow sad circles. "Tell me a better story," she said.

I wanted to peel off her fuzzy striped socks, rub the misery from the arches of her delicate bony feet, wiggle each pearly-pink nail-polished toe. But I didn't dare. So I told her about the girl but not what happened after.

I told her how the girl lived in the branches under a canopy of flowing gossamer sheers as thin and delicate as bees' wings. I told her how we picnicked, the food we ate: little cucumber and egg salad sandwiches on buttered white bread with the crust cutoff, biscuits with clover honey and strawberries and cream. And wild concoctions of tonic made of bark and flower buds which we sipped from cups fashioned from the folds of oak leaves. I told her the girl had porcelain skin and copper penny hair that had a habit of braiding with the tree's roots. And when this happened, the girl's lips would curl up into a lopsided smile, as if someone had just whispered a joke, a bit of delicious gossip. When she wasn't tangling with the tree, she preferred the upper reaches of its canopy. She'd tease me, crawl out to the furthest reach of a thin branch that I was too heavy to traverse. My frustration. Her laughter, tiny chimes flirting with the wind.

"And did she ever tell you what the trees said?" my brother's wife asked.

Not then, not exactly. It would be years later, many years after we first met. I suppressed a grimace, searching for the right words.

"You loved her, didn't you?" she said playfully, jabbing my thigh with her toes. I wished that I had. I was a boy then. What did I know about love?

"It's been a long day. You should go to bed," I said.

"No, not yet." She arched her back, shifted her hips and sighed, "I'm not sleepy."

We both knew she was waiting for my brother. Around two-ish, the clink of keys in the porcelain dish in the hallway announced his arrival. He glanced at us, waved his hand dismissing any words of greeting, shook his head, mumbled something about Rusty the fuckup who had come to save the day, and slowly climbed the stairs. A few hours later, when my brother's wife heard him showering, she rose from the sofa, stiff-limbed and shaky, to make him a pot of coffee. She left behind a scarab-shaped stain, a mirror image of the blackened ruby blemishing the seat of her grey sweatpants.

In the kitchen, she helped my brother wind his yellow tie into a smart double Windsor knot. She relevéd, up onto her tiptoes to give him a kiss. But he was distracted by the convention of crows loitering on his brand new sedan. He rushed out the door, waving his hands, cursing at the bloody motherfuckers. But they didn't budge, just laughed at his passionate outrage, reminding me of the girl in the tree, the last time I saw her, how we parted ways. Red-faced, he marched back into the house, grabbed his keys and suit jacket, gave my sister-in-law a curt peck and said, "Gotta go." The crows clung to their perches, on the roof and the hood and the side-view mirrors as he backed down the entire length of the driveway. Not until my brother sped away did they condescend to spread their wings and, with a riot of caws, took flight.

That Superb Cadaver

By the time I met him, everyone, even the clients, called him Mad Dog, a nickname he acquired simply because his initials, which the firm used to deliver interoffice mail, spelled M.A.D. He was a soft man, with swollen hands and the countenance of an English butler: weak-chinned, sway-backed, protruding belly, superior attitude. The firm had pegged him for a back office slot, something quiet and complicated like patent work. But the nickname became his superpower as he channeled his inner bulldog and adopted the battlefield strategies of his hero, the General "Mad Anthony" Wayne. He carved out a niche for himself, the unpleasant but necessary art of collections.

Given the low billing rate, it was a high-volume operation which required a lot of bodies. Once a month, Mad Dog snared new associates, marched them to the courthouse and trained them to administer judgment debtor's examinations.

Despite his reputation, associates avoided him given the pedestrian nature of collection work. They would rather latch onto a partner with a med-mal or products liability case. I, on the other hand, having already been spoken for by the managing partner, had been secluded in document review hell. I spent my days responding to requests for production, researching rules of civil procedure and writing angry motions to compel. I wanted to get out of the office and onto the street. On the way to the firm's library, I would wander past Mad Dog's office, hoping he'd look past his stack of files and notice me. Finally, he did.

"Cis!" he said making a casting motion and then reeling me in like a fish.

Pressing my palm to my chest, I mimed who me? Then grinned. I said, "Dog!"

He frowned, pointed at the speaker phone then waved me in. A tremor of uncertainty skittered up my spine as I stepped forward. What made me think I could joke with Mad Dog? He picked up the receiver, switched off the speaker, and swiveled his leather chair away from me.

I sat, feeling like a kid summoned to the principal's office. The one who pulls the fire alarm then discovers she didn't want the attention after all. I crossed my legs, right over left. Pumped my foot up and down. Switched legs. A tiny run in my pantyhose leached out from the plane of my foot. I wondered if I had clear nail polish stashed in my briefcase to stop the fraying.

His office walls boasted diplomas and bar admission certificates, and a reproduction of a painting depicting The Battle of Fallen Timbers, a romantic rendition of soldiers on horseback plunging bayonets into Indians.

Two toy soldiers and a cannon on wheels guarded the corner of his tidy desk. Mad Dog turned around just as I was testing the cannon's wheels across my palm.

"Ever been to the courthouse?"

"No," I said. He plucked the cannon from my hand and replaced it with a file.

"Let's go then."

"Now?"

"Yep. I'll tell you the battle plan on the way. The deadbeats will already be sworn in," he said as he grabbed his umbrella. "You can't feel sorry for them."

I nodded in agreement.

We walked swiftly down the hallway to my office to grab my overcoat. Embarrassed by the calamity of my desk, open books stacked three high, legal pads and highlighters, stacks of files lined the perimeter of the floor, my hands waded into the contents of my desk drawer, pushing aside aspirin, parking tickets, a toothbrush, a birthday card I never mailed, until I found the polish. I shoved it into my pocket as we walked out the door.

All eighteen floors down the elevator, with people getting on and off, Mad Dog preambled rapid fire bullets of information.

"They'll tell you that they couldn't afford an attorney. Didn't know if they failed to respond to the complaint within thirty days that a default judgment would be entered. They'll whine about how the particulars are not right, the interest and whatnot. They'll want to tell you how they got sick and lost their jobs and couldn't pay their hospital bills because they have no insurance. That their spouse died."

We waded through the lobby of the Toledo Edison Building. Mad Dog executed a quarter turn with military parade precision and looked me square in the eyes.

"Remember," he said. "You're not there to listen to their sob stories. You're there to be a detective. To find the money to pay off their debts. They all have something stashed somewhere. Savings accounts, cookie jars, boats, a quarter acre of farm land, Aunt Gertie's car they just inherited. If they squirm, remind them about the oath."

We pushed through the circular doors spilling out into the plaza.

Despite his portly stature, I had trouble keeping up with Mad Dog as we strode towards the courthouse. Constrained by the tight cylinder of my navy blue pencil skirt, I had to take two short strides for every one of his. My patent leather pumps were no match to his large wing tips, which splayed out more like duck feet than paws. Once, we had to stop while I pried a heel out of the sidewalk grating. The run in my hose inched up past my ankle bone.

"And don't forget to ask them if they have any cash on hand. They will of course. For parking, for the bus, for a hot dog lunch. When they pull it out of their pathetic little pockets or their bag lady purses, take it."

As we approached the courthouse, he said, "By the way, you don't look like a lawyer. So use that to your advantage. Just smile, do that eye winking thing that you do and ask nicely. They'll spill their guts because you have that everyone's-little-sister look."

That my appearance could be advantageous was a revelation. People usually mistook me for a high school student visiting dad for the afternoon. Clients meeting me for the first time asked me to hang up their coats, thinking I was a secretary. I always shrugged and complied.

It was my first stint at the courthouse, but I didn't have time to admire the domed edifice, Roman arches, Corinthian columns, or the oxidized copper statue of William McKinley standing sentry. There was no time to examine the frogs carved into its sandstone walls. Mad Dog hustled me in through the Adams Street entrance. When I paused a moment to stare at the tiled frog mosaic under my feet, Mad Dog grabbed my elbow and steered me towards Judge Hartley's courtroom.

"Interesting but not relevant," he said. "Let's save the Black Swamp and Frog Town history lesson for another time, shall we?"

We had only one judgment debtor to examine that day. The bailiff called the case, Toledo Building Supply v. Csonka. Mr. Csonka raised his hand to be sworn in and limped from the courtroom into the hallway and toward the wooden chairs reserved for the daily shakedown.

Mr. Csonka looked relieved when he realized I was conducting the exam. He was a thin wiry man, with bushy eyebrows and a mop of black unruly hair graying at the temples. His nose was crooked and I wondered how he'd broken it. His gray slacks, shiny with hot iron marks, clung to the laces of his steel-toed work boots. His hand was warm when he shook mine.

"Nice to meet you, young lady," he said.

Mr. Csonka told me he was a construction worker from Sylvania. He had fallen from the third story scaffolding, broke his leg in three places, and nearly obliterated his ankle. He was held together by pins, and by now, eighteen months later, he was just beginning to walk without a cane. He was in rehab when the complaint came and his wife, what with six kids and a broken husband, she just couldn't handle the business side of things. I nodded. I listened to his story.

"I'm so sorry Mr. Csonka. How do you think you are going to pay for this?"

"Well, young lady, I can't really say for sure."

"Do you own your house? Can you just tell me the name of your bank, the account number, your social security number?"

He paused while I wrote it all down on my yellow legal pad.

"Do you have a car? Any valuables? What about your wife? Does she have a checking or savings account?"

He told me about his work truck with the flat tires that he'd paid off sometime in the seventies, his hammers, wrenches, collection of screwdrivers, the array of drill bits and other sundries. With pride he told me about his special tool belt, which took ten years to purchase. His wife had a little savings from selling crocheted toilet paper covers and quilts. They were very beautiful, I should come to the church where she sells them on Sundays to see. His wife would love me and would want me to have one.

He told me how his family had immigrated long before the First World War. They were part of the first wave of Hungarians to settle in Toledo's Birmingham neighborhood. He told me the names of his children and showed me their pictures.

Behind me, Mad Dog watched, supervising my efforts. He began to fidget. He coughed. I thought I heard him say, "Ask about the cash."

I hesitated. Again, the muffled cough and the whisper. "Ask about the cash."

"Mr. Csonka?"

"Yes?"

"Have you brought any cash here with you today?"

"Of course. I always have a little cash."

Mad Dog kicked my chair.

"How much?"

"Well, let me see. I spent a few dollars on the bus, and a newspaper, and a coffee. The courthouse coffee tastes a little burnt…"

"So how much then, Mr. Csonka? Can you pull it out and count it?"

He crossed his arms. Mr. Csonka's face, formerly a smooth open plain, cracked then splintered into a hundred red pock marks.

Mad Dog kicked the back of my chair again.

"Mr. Csonka, may I remind you about the oath you took earlier? The one where you placed your hand on the bible and swore to tell the truth about your assets? Where you promised to tell the truth so that we can determine how you are going to pay off the judgment?" I shifted uneasily in my chair and began to perspire. A damp rash of sweat clung to the collar and underarms of my polyester blouse.

Mr. Csonka pulled out his wallet again, thumbed past the photos of little Benjie and Claire, Michael, Jonny, Suzi and Petal. Into my left palm, he counted ten ones, a five and a twenty.

"Thirty-five dollars."

"Ok. Thirty-five dollars." I wrote down the amount on my legal pad. Thirty-five dollars in cash.

"Thank you, Mr. Csonka. I will apply this thirty-five dollars to your…" I flipped through the pages of the file, paused my finger on the amount, "your ten thousand dollar debt."

I stashed my legal pad and the money into my briefcase and stood up to go.

"Are you kidding me? My wife, she gave me that money this morning. From the button box. How am I going to get home? How am I going to buy groceries for tonight's supper?"

"I'm sorry Mr. Csonka. I really am."

"Please Lady," Mr. Csonka clenched his fist. "Please. At least, give me back enough money for the bus."

I hesitated. I reached into my briefcase to fish out Mrs. Csonka's crochet money.

Mad Dog stood up and grabbed my arm, whispered in my ear. "Time to go now, Cis."

"I'm sorry, Mr. Csonka." A lump swelled in my throat. I felt nauseous.

Mr. Csonka laughed. It started small. At the back of his throat. It was a raspy, phlegmy coughing sound. Like an old engine that refused to turn over. And it grew until it exploded into a large bellowing howl. The bailiff, who was leaning against the wall some distance away, stood up and sauntered over. His gun and night stick at his side.

"You know what, lady," said Csonka. "With all your questions? You forgot to ask me the most important one."

"Excuse me?"

"The meaning of my name. That's what you forgot to ask me. It's Hungarian, you know." His voice trailed off as he reached into his pocket and pulled out a pack of cigarettes.

"I always thought it was strange. That it didn't fit. Not my life. Not even after the accident. But now, you lady, you did this to me and now it fits. You look, you find. You see what you do to me. I hope you can sleep at night."

The bailiff stood between me and Mr. Csonka.

"Is there a problem, Ma'am?"

"No. No problem," I said.

To Mr. Csonka, he said, "You can't smoke in here, sir. Besides, those things will kill you."

"It doesn't matter. Ask her. I'm dead already."

Ω

Afterwards, Mad Dog took me to Dyers Chop House for a victory lunch.

"What'd I tell you?" Mad Dog said as he plunged a bloody square of steak into his mouth.

As he chewed, he sawed off a new bite, dipped it into his baked potato smothered in sour cream and chives. He set his fork down just long enough to swirl his glass of Burgundy and took an indelicate sip. He had a little mouth. It left a prim mark of food and saliva on the rim.

I had ordered "just a salad" but Mad Dog wouldn't have it. "She'll have the prime rib, too," he said to waiter. To me he said, "You think football players have just a salad after a game? No. They eat meat. They need protein. It repairs and builds muscle after a battle. And that's what you just did. Battle. You did good, Cis. Besides, when I go to the gym, I see you at aerobics dancing around in one of those leotard thingies. You could stand to put on a pound or two."

I pictured Mad Dog working out in the weight room above the aerobics room, curling twenty-five-pound weights, leering down onto the wooden floor below, watching me and twenty other women grapevining to the Bangles, *Manic Monday* with arms cartwheeling, punching. Or twenty women on their backs, raising hips, to Michael Jackson. *Beat It.* Up and down, pelvic tilts. Open crotches pulsating. It only took a second to wrap the vision in butcher paper, tie it with twine. I threw it in the box, at the back of my mind.

The prime rib arrived on a platter swimming in its bloody juices. A thick ribbon of fat hugged the curves of the slab of meat. I stabbed it with my fork. I carved it into thirty-five bite-sized pieces, one for every dollar I stole from Mr. Csonka.

Mad Dog nodded at my plate and then raised his wine glass in salute. "And the sky was watching that superb cadaver," he said pausing for effect, "blossom like a flower."

"What?"

"Baudelaire. 'The Carcass.' You should read it. It's relevant."

When we left Dyers, I expected to see Mr. Csonka loitering on the corner, working the late lunch crowd for a few nickels and dimes, bus fare. I wondered how he had gotten home. I was still new to Toledo, unfamiliar with the neighborhoods. Could he walk home from here? Would he have to cross a highway? I remembered his limp and the pins that were holding him together. I wondered what Csonka meant. The run in my pantyhose had spread like an infection toward my thigh.

Ω

The next morning, the mailroom delivered a legal-size envelope with a note attached: "Compliments of Mad Dog." Inside I found the photocopy of the Baudelaire poem. A man and his lover go for a walk and find an animal of some sort, lying on its back, dead long enough to smell, its legs raised in the air, paralyzed in the grip of rigor mortis. Or, as Baudelaire says, like a beautiful whore. There are flies and maggots and worms. A dog lays in wait, ready to snatch its bones. All that ugly decay while the sky watches it blossom like a flower.

I thought I might get sick. The room spun. Heat prickled my face and the back of my neck. Did Mad Dog get some perverse sexual pleasure from ripping people apart? Humiliating them in their darkest moments? Was the destruction of a man's honor like some climax? And what was my role in all of this? I crumpled the poem and threw it away.

A few weeks after my initiation, Mad Dog developed a nasty bout of gout. He unlaced his Brooks Brothers' wingtips and yanked off his argyles to reveal an angry swollen big toe. I was on my way to the law library when he spotted me striding past his office.

"Hey Cis," he said. "Got a minute?"

Of course, I didn't. Wallenda was waiting for a brief, Mr. Hillcrest wanted me to find a few sixth circuit cases, and Bennett wanted interrogatory responses to an asbestos complaint. Plus, I had to "coach" our stupid firm softball game which required me to lug coolers full of ice and beer, rubber bases and an assortment of bats to a neighborhood baseball field on the other side of town.

"Sure," I said.

His naked foot sat propped up on a stack of case books. I tried not look at it, the tuft of hair sprouting from his gigantic red knob of a toe.

"Doctor says I have to stay off the foot for a few weeks. So, you've been enlisted." He patted the six-inch stack of files on the top of his otherwise empty desk. "Thirty-five new collection cases. The exams are already scheduled. All you have to do is show up. You already know what to do."

As I gathered the bundle in my arms, Mad Dog said, "Oh, and do you mind getting me a tonic water? And some ice, for the toe?"

During Mad Dog's convalescence, Mr. Csonka was summoned to the courthouse three more times. By the hospital, the lumber company, then the mortgage and loan. All clients of Strathy, McMahon. Each time, the file landed on my desk. While my peers became experts in complex product liability cases, jetting off to LA and Houston, Toronto and New York City, I became an expert on Mr. Csonka, his mounting debts, his dwindling assets and collateral. And even though the firm possessed a typewritten list of it all, knew what he had and didn't have, I proceeded with every exam since each generated billings for the firm. I no longer needed my tutor Mad Dog as an escort. I no longer marveled at the Corinthian columns or the tiled frog mosaic.

Mr. Csonka no longer offered pictures of his kids or discussed his wife's crocheted blankets and tea cozies. No tearful accusations. Just cold silent contempt.

At night, when the hallways of Strathy, McMahon were quiet except for the sound of the custodian's vacuum and my stomach agitating for food, I searched the law library shelves. I found telephone books dating back to the fifties, racks of newspapers, mostly *The Toledo Blade* and *The Wall Street Journal* but also the *Detroit Free Press* and the *Akron Beacon Journal,* and five foreign language dictionaries: two French, one German, one Spanish, and one Russian. But no Hungarian dictionary.

I knew where the librarian kept her stash of Twizzlers and was prepared to grab some from her upper right-hand drawer when I noticed a stack of history books she acquired for Mad Dog, including *The Life and Death of Mad Anthony Wayne.*

I was too tired to be interested in Mad Dog's reading fancies. I grabbed a fistful of black licorice and left. So I didn't read that Mad Anthony Wayne met his demise from a severe case of gout. I didn't read that he died in Erie, Pennsylvania, and was buried there. I didn't read that his son, Isaac, and his friend Dr. Wallace exhumed his body thirteen years later so it could be taken home to eastern Pennsylvania. I didn't learn that the body was remarkably well-preserved and still clung to most of its flesh, except notably the leg infected with gout. I didn't learn that the body was too large to haul in the two-wheeled sulky they had brought, so Dr. Wallace chopped his body into pieces, boiled the flesh from the bones and transported the clean skeleton home for a second burial.

Later, when I was no longer coaching the softball team or fetching bags of ice, well into my second year, issuing orders to a new crop of first years and nearly over Mr. Csonka and his wife's tea cozies, I found a Hungarian English dictionary at a garage sale. The musty yellow pages smelled of paprika and regret. I thumbed through the Cs until my index finger landed on Csonka. Maimed. Defective. Mutilated.

It was Friday morning, an hour or so past midnight, when the giant pandas arrived trailing vapors from the ancient Qionglai Mountains. Nine thousand miles. Thirteen time zones. The curve of the earth turning early afternoon into almost yesterday.

Sarah huddled on the tarmac with the newscasters, cameramen, zoo officials, and a few others lucky enough to nab a press pass; together their heads craned skyward. For a moment, Sarah saw the Tibetan Plateau in the contrails: snow-capped peaks, deep river gorges, jagged slopes so green that the air tasted like moss. And then bamboo forests, then tumbling waterfalls, then yak-herding peasants walking like gods amidst the fog and mist and clouds.

The vision vanished, dissolving in a shimmer as the cargo plane landed at the Toledo airport. The runway skirted by parched cornfields, crumbling strip malls, Loma Linda's Mexican cantina, and the Ohio turnpike.

The panda keepers emerged from the hull dressed like prom dates in wrinkled white dinner jackets, black trousers, and thin black ties. Blinded by the television cameras and flash bulbs, the delegation stood dutifully for their photo op as baggage-handlers, mindful of their audience, gingerly unloaded two enormous dog crates with the drugged and oblivious pandas curled inside like yin and yang. They were less careful with the other cargo, cursing as they heaved twenty-six containers of panda souvenirs: stuffed toys, yo-yos, magnets, salt and pepper shakers, neckties, pins, tea cups, shower curtains, and toilet seat covers.

The second plane, the luxury airliner, carried the lawyers and politicians who had been holed up in a Shanghai hotel, smoking cigars, wrangling the law at the tricky intersection of conservation and commerce. They parsed the difference between goodwill loans and commercial exploitation. Tracked panda estrus with charts and calculators. With endless shots of baijiu knifing their throats, they exchanged toasts with their Chinese counterparts. *Ganbei!* thrummed in their morning-after hangovers.

Sarah's husband, Eddie, was one of them. He'd been away for two months with only a handful of telephone calls, hurried nothings full of static, to bridge the distance. She hadn't bothered to tell him about the little rosebud that had been blooming ever so briefly inside her incompetent womb. Sarah knew he had given up the idea of a family as the thing that would propel him forward with the firm. He was banking on the pandas now.

Eddie descended the airstairs. Flanked by senators, the governor, and the secretary of state, Eddie swaggered to the bouquet of microphones. He didn't let on that the WWF had challenged the validity of the zoo's import permit, that they were scheming to confiscate the pandas, to shut the whole thing down, that millions of dollars hung in the balance. He cleared his throat and leaned in, congratulated the team for making the impossible possible. Using his best Mr. Miyagi impersonation, he said, with a clipped cadence and a deep gravel that rumbled at the back of his throat, "Man who catch fly with chopsticks can do anything."

Sarah would have cringed but she had her eye on the keeper, the tall one, Quentin, who she'd meet later at the Panda Gala. She was distracted by the roguish wisp of black hair that strayed over his brow, and the hint of a smile on his lips.

Sarah pulled her sweater tighter, the cool night air digging deep into the vacant hollow of her belly. In a few days, the temperatures would climb with an unrelenting persistence. A hundred-year drought on its way. Preachers would pray over the crops. A Sioux medicine man summoned from South Dakota would perform a rain dance. People would swear that the feathers and the tom-toms and the customary chanting produced a momentary drizzle.

Sarah welcomed the heat. She had no garden to tend, no delicate seeds or tender shoots to protect.

When the exhibit opened, Sarah witnessed Nan Nan on display at the zoo. Bleating like a lamb. All those sweaty palms and eager faces pressed up against the plexiglass as the cat-footed bear lumbered, pacing back and forth, finally settling into the furthest corner of the concrete pen, presenting her back to the crowd. Le Le, her male companion, stashed away in separate quarters so they couldn't mate. Sarah could sense the desperation, Nan Nan's need. Eddie sighed when he saw Sarah's mascara running, smudged into half-moon circles that resembled the tear-shaped patches around Nan Nan's eyes.

"What the hell is the matter with you?" Eddie whispered so as not to disenchant his retinue of clients or the ever-vigilant keepers. He handed her a tiny stuffed panda, a consolation prize pinched from the gift shop.

Quentin offered his handkerchief and a behind-the-scenes tour where Sarah could see Nan Nan and Le Le slurp panda gruel and gnaw on bamboo shoots away from the ten-thousand-person-a-day crowd. Where the pair wrestled and rolled and gamboled, climbed ladders, slid down slides, and cuddled on a panda-sized porch swing.

Later, Quentin told her all the panda legends. How they got their spots mourning the shepherdess who died saving a panda cub from a hungry tiger. How they rubbed ashes on their bodies in tribute, rubbing their eyes with their ashy paws, refusing to wash away their grief. How sleeping on a panda pelt encouraged the disappearance of unwanted ghosts, how it also regulated a woman's cycle so she menstruated with the moon. Once, Quentin snuck her into Nan Nan's pen at night. When Sarah combed her fingers through Nan Nan's coarse wooly fur, she felt the splendid heat of possibilities. Of life beyond cages, beyond assumptions and cruel expectations.

Later still, Quentin told her other things while his elegant fingers traced the ridges of her spine. How his Chinese name was Ti-Ling. How her body was like the lush foothills of the mountains. All rhododendron and lavender primrose, thickets of umbrella bamboo. And tree buds swollen, aching for the sun bursts above the clouds. On her back he drew snow leopards, and golden monkeys, and yellow-throated marlins. On her stomach, he drew maps of the meandering Min River and the Great Yangtze.

The heat, a lazy but insistent sampan drifting from morning to night, inched past one hundred degrees.

Eddie was furious when he lost the lawsuit filed by the WWF, hot tears stung his eyes as the pandas and the souvenirs and the keepers left without an apology only one hundred days after they first arrived.

And still Sarah welcomed the heat, remembering stolen moments in the keepers' house, the bungalow purchased by the zoo, its pantry stocked with Uncle Ben's minute rice and Lipton tea bags and canned Chicken Chow Mein manufactured some fifty miles west in Archbold, Ohio.

NORMA FLOATS TOWARD THE CONFERENCE ROOM with the ageless grace of a dancer. Never mind the catheter bag strapped to her thigh, hidden underneath the generous balloon of her silk trousers. She feels like a movie star with the crowd, the camera, the lights and all. Almost Hollywood, if you overlook the peeling wallpaper, a gold damask, its raised textured flowers and leaves vining towards the florescent sky and the stained commercial-grade carpet masquerading as Opera House Red. Holiday Inns have never been glamorous. Even so, someone could have sprung for a better venue since this will surely be her last performance.

Baggins, her lawyer, leads the procession like a dandified gangster in a double-breasted pinstripe and two-toned wingtips. Norma follows, pulling Howard in his little cart. The girl, Tulip, skips alongside. She wears white gloves, a green taffeta dress and a slick ballet bun secured with a tiara. She curtseys to the hotel staff and the stenographer triggering a delighted chorus of chuckles and a smattering of applause before she scrambles up into her chair. She opens up a black patent leather pocketbook she found in Norma's costume closet and pulls out crayons and a folded coloring book.

The defense lawyers, a plague of them, swarm the room, winking their yellow legal pads and chorusing their clicking ink pens, conjuring cicadas in a late summer sundown.

Norma tugs at Baggins' cuff-linked sleeve. "Why are there so many?"

Baggins cocks his head, leans in toward Norma. "All those products we listed in the complaint," he says.

She nods, remembering popcorn poppers, hair dryers, ironing board covers, crockpots, potting soil, baby powder, paneled curtains, wool coats. The vinyl wallpaper she hung in the downstairs powder room, ceiling tiles, cork board in the kitchen. Paints and paste and caulk. Such betrayal. All those homey things, harboring microscopic assassins. But hasn't she always known that domesticity was a killer?

Cecelia Armstrong strides into the room. Baggins hasn't seen her since his days working as a clerk at Strathy, McMahon. She had always been nice to him. Greeted him with a smile and a wink, like they were co-conspirators. She lent him her law school outlines and hornbooks. Coached him through torts and property law. In return, he'd sprint to the courthouse ten minutes to five with a last-minute filing, scrounge up the last can of Diet Coke from the seventeenth-floor kitchen, lug soggy, mouse-infested discovery boxes to her office. Late at night, she'd leave offerings of black licorice and airplane-sized bottles of whiskey on his dented metal desk in the mailroom. But then he made the mistake of asking her out. Left a note on her desk sandwiched between her Bernie Kosar bobble head and biography of Sandra Day O'Connor.

"What the hell is this?" she said, cornering him in the back hallway in between rows of gray filing cabinets. In those days, she always looked off kilter, as if she had just spun out of a tornado with snagged stockings, chipped nail polish, and hair teased into a high-rise rat's nest. Sometimes she wore mismatched shoes, one black, one navy. "I can't go out with you," she shouted. "No one will take me seriously if I go out with the mailroom guy. Don't fuck this up for me. Okay?"

Now, five years later, she wears a tailored black dress, belted at the waist, long sleeved with a high collar. Both he and Norma notice her lean legs and her spotless black patent leather heels.

Yesterday, at Norma's little house on Cherry Street, with the overgrown hedges and yard littered with dandelions and crab grass, Baggins warned Norma that the defense group would choose a woman as lead counsel. Get Norma all relaxed with softball questions, vital statistics, name, age, serial number, that sort of thing and then the others would attack.

"Baggins, never underestimate the cunning, the will, the stamina of a dancer. I wasn't much older than Tulip when I started at the academy. I endured Mam'selle's wicked yardstick, that splintery old thing. She'd give me a crack," she said smacking his arm with her open palm.

"Ouch! Why would she do that?" he said. He rubbed the spot where he sensed a welt blooming.

"To encourage straighter legs. Apparently, I had lazy knees. She'd give me two cracks for a sickled foot." Norma kicked off her satin embroidered mules and pointed her long knobby toes. "This is sickled." She moved her foot a fraction of an inch. "This is not. See the difference?"

Baggins nodded yes even though he didn't. "The beauty is all about the line, Baggins. Can't get it without some bruises and bloodied toes along the way. Sort of like practicing law, is it not?" She patted his arm still stinging from the slap. "Don't worry about me. I can hold my own," Norma said.

But now, as the videographer adjusts his lights and the court reporter sits poised to record her every word, the pinch of tape and weight of the urine bag on her thigh, the plastic tubing tethering her to the oxygen canister, she is not so sure.

Ω

Baggins showed up, the first time, in a rainstorm, droplets splattering his clipboard, smearing the ink. Looking more like the Fuller Brush Man than an attorney in his scuffed shoes and brown suit. Nothing left to do but to invite him in.

Baggins was surprised by the elegance of the place, its grandfather clock, Persian rugs, and oil paintings of what he imagined to be the French countryside. He took off his hat, revealing a bad combover. Norma grabbed the hat, shook off the droplets and hung it on the brass rack next to Howard's gray fedora.

Norma sucked on the end of her tortoise shell cigarette holder. Baggins shifted nervously under her gaze. She wore a black leotard with a scoop neck and three-quarter length sleeves and a piece of fabric that looked like a table cloth wrapped around her slender waist and rounded tummy.

"Young man, there's no excuse for an ugly suit," she said. She tapped the clipboard with the pointed tip of her Holly Golightly. "What is that? The Black List or something? If it is, you're late. McCarthy stopped by about forty years ago."

"No ma'am."

"Don't ma'am me. I don't feel like a ma'am. Do I look like a ma'am?"

Baggins shifted his wet feet. "No ma'am." Baggins thought she looked like a swan.

"Well, speak up. Why are you here? I don't want to buy anything if you're selling. Only invited you in because Tulip and I get lonely sometimes and we like a little bit of company."

Norma laughed, a rumbly phlegmy laugh, what nurses call a productive cough. Followed by a slight wheeze. As if somewhere buried deep within her sternum, below her elegant clavicle, a tiny flute whistled. The sound reminded Baggins of the soft pink belly of a sea shell.

Beyond the vestibule, Baggins could see a little girl arranging China tea cups on the coffee table. She wore a tattered bridal veil and a vintage fur wrap circled around her tiny shoulders, its embrace secured by a triangular fox head biting its own tail.

"Your granddaughter?" he said nodding towards the girl.

"No. Not mine. She's on loan from next door." Norma smiled warmly at the girl and gave a silent directive with a flourish of her hands. "Now who are you and what do you want?"

"My name is Robert Barnum."

"No." She cocked her head. "You don't look like a Barnum." She searched his face. His rumpled suit. "What do you think, Tulip?" She remembered the Hobbit cartoon they watched the Saturday morning before last. "Doesn't he look more like a Baggins?" Tulip looked up and smiled. "Yes. That's it," Norma said. "We'll call you Baggins. So what do want?" She sucked dramatically on her cigarette-less cigarette holder, flared her nostrils, and exhaled an imaginary puff of smoke.

By this time, he was so flustered he didn't object to his new name. He merely responded, "Well actually, I was looking for Mr. Zimmerman."

"Howard?"

Baggins looked down at his clipboard and the list of smeared names. He pulled a pair of thick black glasses from his trouser pocket.

"Yes. Howard Zimmerman. Is he here?"

"Howard is not here as you can see. Why don't you come back tomorrow?" she said handing back his damp hat. "We'll have a cup of tea. Then you can tell me all about that list of yours and why my husband is on it."

Ω

Outside the Commodore Perry conference room, a white poster board on an easel announces the nine AM Zimmerman deposition taking place inside. Oxygen in use. No Smoking. The long, long conference table, propped with water pitchers, glasses, several boxes of tissues, and two microphones, awaits the players.

Baggins pulls out a chair for Norma, helps her sit and scooches her in, being careful not to separate her from the contraption Norma has affectionately christened Howard, a missile-shaped oxygen tank nestled in a caddy on wheels. Strapped to the top is an antique Russian samovar, its copper belly resembling a round face with pinkish green cheeks, its spigot resembling a crooked nose, and its ornate handles suggesting prominent ears. Across the table, three rows deep, sit attorneys in various states of attentiveness. The young female lawyer, mistress of ceremony, Norma's interrogator, introduces herself.

"Mrs. Zimmerman," she says offering her hand. "I'm Cecelia Armstrong. I see you brought a fine counselor with you here today." She smiles and winks at Baggins. "He's one of the best."

"So I hear," Norma says with droll inflection. Norma notices the smile and the wink and Baggins' flushed face. She notices the lawyer's long neck, the flutter of her hands reaching for the necklace at the nape of her neck. "And you, my dear? You look familiar. Was it Swan Lake down at the Rep?" Norma asks.

"No. Wasn't me," Cecelia says. "I always begged for ballet lessons. It just never worked out."

"Pity. You have the facility for it," Norma says. "You would have made a beautiful Odile."

Cecelia looks at Baggins for clarification. Baggins shrugs.

"The black swan, dear," Norma says. "The black swan."

Baggins clears his throat. "Let's proceed, shall we?"

Norma adjusts the cannula, the rubber T-shaped tube that sits in her nose. Only the faintest lines about her mouth and eyes suggest the tug of seventy some years.

"How are you feeling today, Mrs. Zimmerman?" Cecelia asks. There's a smudge of lipstick on Norma's teeth. Cecelia hands Norma a tissue and silently rubs her own teeth with her forefinger.

"Fine, just fine," Norma says swiping the tissue across back and forth until Cecelia nods her approval. Norma reaches for the pitcher of water but the tube constricts her movement. Baggins pours a glass and hands it to her. Norma takes a sip.

Norma wants to say, *Isn't that why we are here? So I can tell you that I'm NOT fine?* Norma says she is fine not because she is expected to say fine, or because that's what ladies do or because yesterday, during depo prep, Baggins cautioned her to "tone it down a bit," or because a trip to the doctor means the mortgage will be left unpaid. All of which are true. She says she is fine because her audience demands it. Norma never let a broken toe, a bout with pneumonia, even a death in the family interfere with a performance.

"If at any time you need a break, let me know and we will take a break. If there is a question you don't understand or you need me to repeat it, let me know," Cecelia says. "Don't guess. If you don't know the answer, say I don't know. Even though we have a videographer here today, we need you to answer each question with words, even if it's a simple yes or no, you need to verbally say yes or no. The court reporter cannot record a nod or a shake."

Cecelia performs her opening monologue with efficiency, her head tilted just so. Norma can picture her practicing in front of the mirror, each word sliding out like a tendu performed at the barre.

Extend and point. Repeated over and over, to build strength, perfection. Muscle memory. Norma admires her discipline.

"Do you understand why you are here today?" Cecelia says.

"This is a dying deposition is it not? Isn't that what you call it? That's why you got all these extra bells and whistles? Because I'm likely to croak before this three-ring circus gets to court."

The attorneys are unmoved, just stare at her or look down at their legal pads, but Norma can tell she has gotten under Cecelia's skin. Cecelia pauses. Pours herself a water. Ice cubes and lemon slices plop into the glass.

"I'll ask the majority of questions, then these gentlemen can follow up," she says. She tucks a curl behind her ear. "For the record, did you bring anyone here with you today?"

"Baggins, I mean Mr. Barnum, my lawyer. Tulip, and Howard here." Norma gives Howard a pat on his steely cold torso. Her thin wedding band produces a tinny clank. "You really should be a little less stoic," she tells Howard as she laughs her gravelly laugh which turns into a full-fledge coughing fit that lasts at least three minutes and produces a half dozen rusty sputum-stained tissues.

Tulip colors while the rest of the room, including Baggins, looks horrified. Cecelia directs the videographer to stop taping during the maelstrom. Baggins vigorously objects. When the coughing stops, Cecelia suggests a break. She reaches for the used tissues. Baggins uses the tip of his pen to push them directly in front of Norma, making sure that they are within the camera's frame.

"If we stop this interrogation every time I cough, we'll be here till next Tuesday," Norma says.

"Very well," Cecelia says and proceeds to ask every question that Norma and Baggins already answered in the interrogatories—all the info clearly listed in the complaint. Norma states and spells her name for the record. Norma Zimmerman. She had been a Merriweather before she got married, but most people knew her by her stage name. Zelda. Norma is a perfectly good name, but it doesn't really dazzle in marquee lights. Her birthday? Sometime in 1912. Her address? 140 Cherry Street. Married? Yes. Howard Zimmerman. For nearly fifty years. She strokes the missile-shaped canister beside her.

Cecelia pauses, looks down at her notes. "Mrs. Zimmerman. Is your husband sitting here with you today?"

Norma leans forward. "Do *you* think my husband is sitting here today?"

"Please answer the question Mrs. Zimmerman."

Norma knows what the lawyer is trying to do and she isn't going to fall for it. "No. My husband isn't sitting here."

Cecelia stares at her for a long time. Norma stares back.

"Do you have any children?"

"Children? No. No children." *Not unless you count this alien growing inside me*, Norma thinks. She's not supposed to talk about the other cancer, the one invading her womb. She had never been blessed with a child. Just a few sad miscarriages, then nothing. Then her monthlies stopped. She thought she was like Sarah in the bible, when she started bleeding again, long after the change. After being barren for so many years and early menopause to now harbor a wave of crimson blooming between her legs, a sure sign of fertility in her mind. Made her want Howard with an intensity she'd long forgotten. Understandably, Howard was confused and, as hard as he tried, he couldn't satisfy her needs. "Why now?" He sobbed. With disbelief, they both stared at his limp apparatus.

Despite his failure, she could feel the baby growing, from the first familiar feeling of the egg burrowing into the tender lining of her uterus, to the nausea and the fatigue. A little pea, a nut, an egg, and then a fist so rock-hard she could feel it protruding from her lower abdomen. And the feathery feeling, that arrived after the fist, the one that she mistook for quickening, the flutter of tiny hands and tiny feet, a sure sign that she was incubating a performer, and then the pregnancy heartburn, all of which lasted well beyond nine months.

Ω

The second time Baggins knocked on the door at 140 Cherry Street, he arrived in the same suit and scuffed shoes. The ink on the clipboard had dried. Norma greeted him with a kiss. He wondered whether he should wipe off the waxy red marks her lipstick left on his cheek as he took in her black turban, the dressing gown with the leopard-print collar and the knotted string of opera pearls. As Norma ushered him to the chintz sofa covered in pink cabbage roses and blue peacocks, she ordered him to take off his shoes. She produced a shoeshine kit, a round wooden box with a variety of polishes, a flannel cloth and shoe brush.

"I can't think with those shoes of yours screaming at me. Hand them over." She opened the lid of the box, fished around the flat round tin jars of paste, bringing up cordovan, black, mahogany, mid-tan before settling on brown. "You know, Baggins," she said, "everything you need to know about a person, you can learn from their footwear." Norma brushed dirt from the sides and soles of his loafers. "Take your socks, for example: black, no nonsense, reserved, safe. Neutral really. But scuffed, unpolished shoes? Tells me you're hesitant, lack confidence. You lack polish. No pun intended."

She dipped the flannel cloth into the tin and proceeded to dab brown paste on the leather upper, rubbing brisk circles as she talked. "Ballerinas are the only people who can wear scuffed footwear with impunity." She told him about her beautiful handmade pointe shoes. "A dancer can search a lifetime for the right shoe and once you find one, you pray good health and longevity to its maker. Mine were made by Nikolai in Moscow. They'd arrive in a nest of tissue, perfect pink satin vessels of torture. Then I would take a hammer to them, slam them in doors. Used a fork to rake ridges in the leather soles, I'd used Papa's razor blade to cut off the satin on the toe boxes." She buffed the toes and sides of the loafers, a swift back and forth with the horse hair brush, holding up her shoe-puppeted hand, admiring her handiwork.

Norma looked up at the grandfather clock which chimed half past. "Well, that does it for today. I need to get Tulip up from her nap. Do come back tomorrow."

This went on for a half dozen more visits with no hint of Howard Zimmerman on the premises. Norma wearing feather boas, or harem pants, or a gold lame evening gown. Norma lecturing Baggins on everything from shirts (white button downs, one hundred percent cotton, no polyester blends and never, ever short-sleeved) to hairstyles (banish the comb-over, embrace the bald.)

"You know women find bald men attractive, all that testosterone makes them very virile. Not many people know this but before I met Howard—I danced off Broadway with Yul Brynner. Bald and Russian, now that's a combination."

On the day that Baggins finally confessed the provenance and purpose of the list, Norma invited him over for lunch. He brought a grocery store bouquet of white carnations tipped in green for St. Patrick's Day and a pint of mint chocolate chip ice cream for Tulip. They feasted on Spaghettios served in Wedgewood soup bowls. Sipped milk from crystal wine glasses. Tulip showed Baggins how to drape his white linen napkin on his lap before reaching for the ornate silver spoon to the far right of his plate.

After supper, as Norma called it, Tulip danced and marched to a crackling record of the London Symphony Orchestra performing Stravinsky's Circus Polka. She pulled both Norma and Baggins to their feet until they were all three holding hands and skipping in a circle. Discordant blasts of French horns and tubas flirted with tip-toeing piccolos and clarinets. When the needle skipped to the end, Norma hugged Tulip, praising her performance.

"You are a very talented little elephant, my darling," Norma said clapping. She explained that Balanchine had choreographed a ballet for the circus. "Imagine, fifty elephants in pink tutus. With fifty ballerinas. In Madison Square Garden. In 1942. Nothing like a spectacle to make people forget a war is going on."

Over ice cream, Baggins confessed that he had bought the list for a thousand dollars from a mass tort outfit—a large out-of-town law firm that staged tractor trailer-sized health screenings. The men on his clipboard never got evaluated for one reason or another. The outfit assured him that he could quadruple his investment if he signed up the people on this list.

"Seems like a lot of money for bunch of names," said Norma.

"It's kinda like buying salvage," Baggins said. "You repackage junk and it's suddenly worth something."

Baggins admitted that he didn't have the pedigree for the fancy law firms downtown. He had gone to night school, finished in the bottom half of his class. He had been a mailroom clerk for a while, then a process server and a weekend janitor at the mall. He passed the bar on the first try but that didn't seem to matter to the gatekeepers, so he was on his own. The list was his investment in his practice. He'd already signed up thirty potential plaintiffs. They all seemed to be healthy but, in this type of litigation, it didn't matter. Companies settled hundreds of cases, *en masse*, just to avoid a huge payout to that one case that's legit.

"So, if Mr. Zimmerman would like to sign up, we could go to the clinic, get some x-rays, see how the lungs are working," Baggins said. He looked up the staircase hoping to catch a glimpse of him. "He did work at the factory, right?" He used his fingers as a rake to smooth the wisps of hair that had come unmoored during the circus dance.

"Baggins, it's time we did something about that flop top of yours."

Baggins didn't even wince when Tulip presented a tray of assorted scalping implements: scissors, straight razor, strop, oil, and shaving cream.

Ω

"I'm not sure that I understand your question," Norma says to Cecelia.

"Were you offered remuneration? Was this suit filed under false pretenses? In other words, do you have a valid reason for filing this suit?"

"Lung cancer is why I am here," Norma says, tugging at the cannula, the oxygen suddenly too cold for her nose. "You know, because of all that damn asbestos everywhere. It's ubiquitous. Have you planted any geraniums lately? That crap is in the potting soil for god's sake."

"There seems to be some discrepancy in your medical records." Cecelia looks over at Baggins, eyebrows raised, not even the hint of a smile or her charming wink. "I am presenting for your review two documents that are substantially the same except for the final paragraph. I have marked them as Deposition Exhibit A and Deposition Exhibit B." Cecelia pushes the exhibits across the table, one set towards the stenographer and one set towards Baggins. Baggins reaches for the records and shoves them in between the pages of his legal pad without looking at them.

"Let's take a break, shall we?" Baggins says.

Ω

Auditioning for the Gridiron was Norma's idea.

"All you need is a pair of tap shoes."

Tulip produced a pair from the costume closet. Two-toned wingtips. Men's size 11. Black with a white handlebar mustache between the toe cap and the bottom rung of eyelets.

"I don't know, Norma. I'm not a tap dancer. I was really hoping we could talk about Howard today."

"Don't be ridiculous. Everyone's a tap dancer, Baggins. They just don't know it. Even Howard tap danced in the day."

Baggins accepted Tulip's gift. He turned them over, examined the triangular metal disks screwed into the heels and toes. He clicked the soles together producing a timid snap.

"Like you mean it, man," Norma ordered. "Like you're smacking erasers."

Baggins complied. The crack was explosive. Like a single shot fired in the woods.

The local bar association hosted the Gridiron every year roasting the headlines and the big names in the legal biz. A vaudevillian show of inside legal jokes, Broadway show tunes, and dance routines performed exclusively by lawyers. Clients and prospective clients from businesses all over the city attended, as did politicians, restaurateurs, and local religious leaders. The proceeds went to charity. But the attorneys reaped the spoils. It was an occasion where deals were made, alliances formed. Baggins couldn't afford the ticket price. But his attendance could be purchased with a performance.

There was no time to spare with auditions to be held in less than a month. During the day, Baggins drove around the city, knocking on doors, ticking names off his list. Along the way, he picked up other types of work. Simple wills, conveyances, minor traffic offenses, shoplifting charges. Each evening, he ate dinner at Norma's. Over scorched skillet eggs and burnt toast, he reported his minor triumphs. Afterwards, Norma took to her sofa, reclining, stretched out like a diva on a fainting couch, most nights in her blue terrycloth robe and fuzzy slippers, with greenish-blue cold cream slathered on her face leaving only her grayish blue eyes and her red lipsticked lips exposed. Baggins helped Tulip tie on her own little pair of black Mary Jane taps. Norma directed from her perch, "See that Persian rug over there? It was a gift from a sultan. Pull it up and you'll find a lovely parquet floor underneath. Perfect for our lessons."

Baggins moved the coffee table to the corner, a stack of Russian novels sliding off in the process. Little moths fluttered up to the ceiling as he rolled the rug into a tight log and dragged it off to the side. The zig-zag patterned floor was deeply scratched but produced a lovely sound with every clack on its wooden surface. Norma clapped and called out steps. Tulip demonstrated. Baggins followed along.

"Step-ball-change, step-ball-change, chassé to the right, chassé to the left, shuffle brush, shuffle drag, slide, tap-tap, tap-tap, tap-tap, stomp."

Baggins loved the syncopated rhythms; they were not only soothing, but he found the percussive patterings of his feet helped him think.

Away from the little house on Cherry Street, when he was reading the fine print of a contract a client had been goaded into signing, or reading tissue thin pages of regulations, Baggins discovered a five-minute session of soft shoe cleared the cobwebs in his head, brought clarity to the jumble of legalities. Norma and Tulip were pleased with the progress of their protégé. It was no surprise when Baggins returned from the audition not only a member of the ensemble but also as an understudy for the lead dance solo.

Baggins had long suspected that Mr. Zimmerman no longer resided at the house on Cherry Street. If he ever lived there at all. In all the framed pictures of circus clowns and pink tutu'ed elephants, feather-headed follies girls in character shoes and cherry-cheeked men in white tuxedos and tails, there was not a single picture of Howard.

Baggins could have gone to the library to look up the obituaries. Or to the courthouse to see if there was a probated estate or a marriage license. He could have done a title search to see who owned the house. He could have done a lot of things including investigate the whereabouts of Tulip's mother. At some point, he stopped asking about Mr. Zimmerman altogether.

With the commencement of Gridiron practice and his growing book of business, Baggins scaled back his visits to once a week, usually on Sundays. Norma seemed a little gray, a little less energetic. She could barely lift the pot of hard-boiled eggs she cooked for Tulip to decorate for Easter. He urged her to lay down while he poured vinegar into bowls fizzing with yellow, pink, green, and blue tablets. By the third Sunday, he pulled up in his rusty Ford hatchback and found the mailbox stuffed. He wrestled out coupon fliers, five days of the *Toledo Blade*, and a clump of bills. As he walked to the front stoop, a letter fluttered to the ground. He reached down to grab it. It appeared to be a Social Security check addressed to Howard P. Zimmerman at 140 Cherry Street.

Ω

Cecelia Armstrong follows the echoing tap tap tapping to the hotel's indoor pool. Her whole body instantly absorbs the moist heat as she opens the door. She knows her hair will soon be a frizzy mess. She reaches up to smooth it anyway and continues in. The chlorine smell reminds her of long-forgotten summers. She navigates the maze of tables and lounge chairs towards a coiled blue hose, long-handled cleaning gadgets, a lifesaver, and Baggins.

"Practicing for the Gridiron? I hear you're really good," she says.

He holds up a finger, pantomiming just a minute. Shuffles through a few combinations. He slides to a stop. "What's up?"

"I like what you did with your hair," she says.

Baggins rubs the back of his scalp and smiles. "You like the new me?"

Cecelia scratches her right ankle bone with her left patent-leathered foot. She doesn't wobble. "Norma needed some assistance in the ladies room. I helped her out."

"Oh. Good." Baggins grabs his blazer draped on a lounge chair.

"She said I have perfect turnout and a natural épaulement—some sort of head tilt and shoulder thing."

"Sounds like Norma," Baggins says as he rolls down his shirt sleeves and buttons his cuffs. "I guess if this whole lawyer thing doesn't pan out, you can go into show biz." He winks at her and she blushes this time.

"I told her I would come find you." She tugs down on the sides of her dress which have inched up mid-thigh. "How long has she had the catheter?"

Ω

"I'm not going," Norma said.

Baggins found Norma propped up in bed, her feet sticking out of a mountain of quilts. Tulip, next to her, in a Strawberry Shortcake nightie, cross-legged, eating marshmallow fluff and peanut butter with a spoon, watching cartoons on the little black-and-white TV in Norma's bedroom. Cold syrup, aspirin, a thermometer, and used tissues littered her bedside table. The room smelled like sweat and nail polish remover. He knew Norma needed to see a doctor. Maybe she just had bronchitis with that cough of hers that had been there since they'd first met.

"Look. I'm either calling an ambulance or you can visit Dr. Abernathy at the clinic where I take all my clients."

"An ambulance will scare Tulip. I won't have it."

"Dr. Abernathy it is then."

Norma scowled. "Tulip just painted my toenails and they need to dry."

"I'll wait."

After Norma changed out of her paper gown and back into her clothes, Dr. Abernathy's nurse ushered Baggins and Tulip into the room to wait out the results. Tulip played with the tongue depressors. Norma sat on the examination table back rigid, fingers digging little holes into the paper cover sheet. Baggins paced the room dodging Tulip's flying popsicle sticks.

Dr. Abernathy knocked before entering the room. He clipped the x-rays up to the light box. "Mrs. Zimmerman, I have some difficult news. The x-rays show numerous spots on your lungs. Pretty sure it's cancer. We'll have to get you to the hospital to do biopsies and what not."

Baggins ran his hand over his newly bald head. His fingers searched among the stubble for the scab where Norma's razor slipped. "The fever and flu like symptoms? Bladder infection. We'll start you on a round of meds, a very strong antibiotic. Do you have any allergies?"

"No," said Norma.

"There's something else." Norma reached out for Baggins. He held her hand. "You have a large immovable mass, possibly uterine cancer. My guess? That's where all the trouble started."

Ω

In the car, on the way back from the hospital, Norma fussed about all the new contraptions and doohickeys she had to contend with. "I always thought I'd go out like Isadora Duncan," she said.

"Who?" Baggins gripped the steering wheel.

"She was a famous dancer. American. But no one appreciated her here. She wasn't exactly a ballerina and there was that thing about liking women as much as men. I don't know why people worry about such things. Love is love. I mean why do I care if Rock Hudson would rather canoodle with a man than Doris Day?" Norma looked over at Baggins to see his reaction. Seeing none she continued, "So, she moved to England around the turn of the century. Traveled the world, mostly Europe and Russia. She was fond of long, flowing hand-painted silk scarfs. And motorcars. The faster the better. Then one

Sunday she went for a joy ride in the French Riviera. All that fabric got caught in the wheels, broke her neck. Just like that. And her head? Almost took the whole thing off."

"That's horrible, Norma."

"More horrible than being tethered to tubes?" she said.

Baggins didn't respond as they pulled into the driveway.

"There's no salvaging this old piece of junk," she said, patting her bloated belly. "I'm not planning on dragging my feet. A good performer always knows when it's time to get off the stage."

Baggins helped Norma and her assorted equipment out of the car.

"We better go tell Howard."

"Just where exactly is Howard?" Baggins opened the front door using Norma's key.

"He's been here all the time." Norma pointed to a Russian samovar, an elaborate two-handled urn with a spout. "It was a joke. One day we were having a spat. He said I might as well put his ashes in the urn—he'd feel comfortable there since he was always in hot water."

Baggins shook his head. "You could have told me, Norma."

She shrugged. "Maybe it's just vacuum cleaner debris. Who really knows where a man goes when he decides to leave." She sank into a chair, kicked off her mules, flexed then pointed her toes. "We're going to have to make provisions for Tulip, Baggins. Little girls on loan are not like returning books to the library. You can't just slip them into the night deposit box."

And so Baggins drafted the complaint.

There was the slight problem of the preliminary diagnosis. Metastatic endometrial cancer. The tumors in her lungs had spread from Norma's childless womb. Not the other way around. Given the medical research at the time, it was unlikely that asbestos was the culprit. The cancerous fist had also moved into Norma's bladder, making the catheter a necessity.

At Norma's direction, Baggins sold the silver, the fine China, and the grandfather clock. With a handful of fresh hundred-dollar bills he paid another visit to Dr. Abernathy. Perhaps the good doctor could be persuaded to slightly modify his report? After all, wasn't it possible that from a lifetime of exposure to household products not to mention handling her husband's work clothes and my god, all those theater curtains on the stages where she danced with Russians, couldn't Norma have inhaled those delicate crystal fibers, mined and used for centuries to thicken paste, and protect firefighters and theaters from going up in flames? Couldn't they have insinuated themselves into Norma's lungs, wreaking silent havoc for decades?

Dozens of named defendants answered the complaint, filed interrogatories and requests for production. Baggins and Norma, single-minded in their endeavor to provide for Tulip, prepared for the deposition.

From the costume closet, Tulip produced the pinstripe suit. Norma had to hem the pleated trousers, but otherwise, they fit just right. Baggins was nearly ready for his big performance.

With a tiny Phillips-head screwdriver, Baggins removed the metal plates from his two-toned oxford tap shoes. He rubbed his meaty thumb across the spaces where the screws used to reside. The holes were barely perceptible.

Ω

Cecelia's question hangs in the air buoyed by chlorine and humid echoes, voices from holidays past, joyful screeches, canon balls, and splashing water.

"Norma's really something, isn't she?" Baggin says.

Cecelia reaches for a long pole with a net attached. She skims the surface of the pool collecting tiny bits of debris, a paper straw wrapper, a purple hair tie, nose plugs, a dented ping pong ball. "She really means a lot to you, doesn't she?"

"Yes." Baggins' voice catches, splinters at the back of his throat. "Yes, she does."

"Do you suppose I should report you to the state disciplinary board?"

"Yes, I suppose you should," he says, putting on his suit jacket. He tugs the cuffs of his white dress shirt a quarter of an inch past his suit jacket sleeves, just the way Norma taught him.

"What will happen to Tulip?"

Baggins shakes his head slowly. "We were going to put everything in a trust, you know, for her care, and dance lessons, college. The situation is complicated but I was hoping she'd come live with me." Baggins picks up his briefcase. "Norma thinks highly of you. Maybe you could take her?"

Cecelia shakes her head no. "Me? Custody of Tulip? Do I look like someone who can provide a home, a future for a child? You know me, Robert. I can barely take care of myself. I wouldn't even know where to begin." She shakes out the gunk she's collected onto the concrete border of the pool, returns the pole to its resting place. "Well, we better get back."

They walk towards the exit and out into the hall. "Do me a favor? Give me a heads up, will you? A little advance notice when you decide what you're going to do?"

"Of course," she says, then stops in the middle of the empty hallway, looks to the left and right then adds, "they're a lazy bunch."

"Who?"

"The peanut gallery, the asbestos circuit attorneys. They just listen for a mention of their client's product at which point they wake up and ask a few questions. Make note that their client will have to pay, at least a little something, so they don't have to spend a fortune going to trial. Otherwise, they have no clue about what's going on. They don't even bother ordering the transcript."

"I don't follow."

Cecelia shrugs her shoulders.

Back at the conference room, Baggins lingers in the threshold, while Norma and Howard and Tulip, already seated, look at him expectantly as they wait for the second act to begin. His shoulders sag from the weight of his responsibility, the enormity of the task before him. Norma straightens her own shoulders—lifts her chin, a cue for Baggins to buck up. He thinks about Mam'selle's wicked stick and adjusts his carriage, takes a deep cleansing breath. Norma gives Tulip a little pat and she jumps out of her chair, skips to the door, and takes his hand.

The Parade of Horribles

JIMMER CAME TO US ONE NIGHT, carried in by the East Wind. A souvenir, more or less, from my father's travels. You would have thought, given the way we fussed over him, that we had found him in a Moses basket floating down the creek at Sand Run Park, a baby instead of a thirteen-year-old on the cusp of becoming a man. He was a darling boy. That's what everyone said. "That Jimmer, he's a darling boy." With his sandy brown curls, a dimple in his left cheek, hazel eyes, and enviable baby-doll lashes. He charmed us with his wide easy grin, his chipped tooth. We claimed him, each of us, even my mother, as one of our own, to our initial delight and later distress. Son, brother, confidant. Savior. He was like the first day of spring—warming our bones with his sunshine, summoning crocuses and clumps of delicate snow drops. Only later would we notice his winter, an icy gray burden he shouldered like a melancholy poet.

My father had been gone for months, off and on, crisscrossing the states, shilling frozen fish and a tangle of something green, spinach perhaps, single servings of slimy diet food that came in pink boxes. He sold these promises of skinny perfection to regional grocery store chains, vitamin shops with cold storage, and a handful of B-list actresses. My father, sworn to secrecy, couldn't reveal their identities but whispered, after his tongue had been loosened by a few Manhattans, that one of those gals might have played, back in the day, a pony-tailed genie in pink harem pants on TV. Somewhere along the way, in Burbank or Bakersfield or maybe Duluth, my father discovered

Jimmer, the son of a former girlfriend, the darling boy with no place to go. So, there he was in our doorway, many airplane miles later, Jimmer in his faded and frayed bell bottom jeans, an army-green duffle bag slung over his shoulder.

"Hey man," he said to all of us, smiling, not the least bit shy. He dropped his duffle bag, stuffed with all his worldly possessions, hugged Mom, Margot, and me. We received the hugs awkwardly at first but melted into his firm insistence.

All these years later, when I remember this moment, my mind conjures Gershwin's "Rhapsody in Blue," the United Airlines version, not the one Jimmer would come to play imperfectly on the piano next door, and not the long symphonic version with the sexy two-and-a-half octave clarinet glissando, with all that anticipation, the slow inevitable climax. Instead, the scene and the music cuts right to the airplane soaring above the clouds and the full orchestra, the bright overlay of horns, the intermittent and urgent piano chords, the triumphant clashing cymbals. The commercial wouldn't come out for another thirteen years, but there it is indelibly seared in my mind as the soundtrack for Jimmer's arrival, because that's the way memory works. The longer you live, it jumbles with specificity.

We had not been expecting my father. If we had, it would not have been with joyful anticipation. We were not Marmee and her girls waiting for Mr. March to come home from the war. In the midst of packing, on that particular day, Margot's hall of fame: her blue ribbons for horseback riding, trophies for speech and debate, her varsity letter and field hockey stick, National Honor Society certificates, the framed newspaper article featuring her standing ovation performance in *Bye Bye Birdie*, we were getting ready to move out of the house on Hudson Street which we had to sell on account of some financial troubles I didn't understand at the time. The house, stately, old-money-grand, white with black shutters, hunter green door, a lion's head door knocker, an orchard for a backyard, stood on a tree-lined avenue just down the way from a historic boarding school. It had been shabby until Mom, single handedly, painted and wallpapered, sewed all the drapes and the bedspreads, refinished and reupholstered garage sale antiques. But in the last few months, Mom sold most of the furniture. We needed the cash and all those fine pieces wouldn't fit in the apartment Mom rented for us on the busy street just off the highway twenty miles away. I cried when Mr. Treadway, the headmaster from said boarding school, exchanged fifty dollars cash for the armchair we called the throne with its fisted paws and the intricately carved dragon on its back, carted it, stumble stepping to his old Wagoneer, and drove away. Our future rewritten, Mom lit a cigarette, laid out the new plans: in a few months, Margot would graduate, head off to a local college, not the prestigious ivy to which she had been accepted. I would finish off sixth grade and be installed in a city school for seventh. I could already feel the tire factory fumes and the car exhaust filling my lungs, constricting my twelve-year-old chest.

Generally, I preferred my father's absences. He was a difficult man, unpredictable from moment to moment, given to tirades, rankled by our imperfections. Not even Margot's hall of fame could stand up to his scrutiny. He picked at each accomplishment until it festered into an open wound: the solitary B on an otherwise perfect report card, finishing second instead of first, being cast as a sidekick instead of the lead. Usually, the point of reentry into the family fold was the worst, when he noticed a pimple, hair that refused to perform like a beauty queen, an extra pound or two. But in the foyer, with Jimmer by his side, he was a different man despite his familiar rumpled three-piece suit. Jimmer had softened him somehow, smoothed his rough edges. Still, Mom was stunned when my father explained that Jimmer would be staying with us, for just a little while, until he figured this thing out. Mom countered, "There's not enough beds now and no room in the new place."

Jimmer broke the silence. "Hang on," he said. "I got you something." He rummaged through his bag and produced a brooch—a floral spray of fake amethysts—for Mom, a French phrase book for Margot. And for me a black eye patch. He showed me the remarkable versatility of the thing, demonstrating on his own head how I could cover one eye to be a pirate or a one-eyed monster called a cyclops or how I could place it in the middle of my forehead like a third eye. I loved it immediately, imagined the possibilities without a hint of foreboding.

"The young man is hungry, Victoria. Fix him a sandwich, will you?"

This is where my faulty memory disappeared Margot and prematurely installed Mrs. Stevens, with her flaming red hair, blue eye shadow, spidery false eyelashes. We wouldn't meet her until years later, but there she was in her white go-go boots and a sleeveless pink sheath dress that revealed her freckled arms. My father draped an arm around her back. Mrs. Stevens emitted a tiny mouse-like giggle so different from her usual boisterous laugh. "Let's fix ourselves a cocktail, shall we?" said my father.

Jimmer picked up his duffle bag and the two of us followed Mom to the kitchen. With little to absorb the sound, our footsteps echoed on the hardwood floors.

For me, a peanut butter and jelly would do, but not for Jimmer. Mom wasn't much of a cook, but she insisted on making a production of Jimmer's first meal with us. Meatloaf and baked potatoes and Bird's Eye frozen squash.

Jimmer hopped up on a wobbly kitchen stool with an avocado green seat and I hopped up on the one next to him, the place I would covet for years. I mostly watched him watching Mom, but I could tell she was having a big think. You could see her working out the situation in her mind while she busied her hands. She preheated the oven to three fifty, scrubbed five russet potatoes. In a mixing bowl, she plopped a pound of ground beef, a cup of Quaker Oats, a few squirts of ketchup and Worcestershire sauce, four cranks each of salt and pepper. My father wandered in to grab a jar of olives and to fill his silver ice bucket and then back to the study where he and Mrs. Stevens, back from the future, intermittently laughed and argued. Mom curtly minced the onion, her eyes teared. She stopped to take a shaky puff of the cigarette balanced on the edge of the kitchen sink, then cracked two eggs into the mess. Jimmer grimaced as she plunged her hands into it, yolk and whites sliming through her fingers as she kneaded.

With each squish, Jimmer's brow furrowed, his stomach groaned. Mom shaped the meat into a loaf, placed it in the oven with the potatoes and set the timer for an hour. She tapped the spent ash from her cigarette, brought it to her coral-lipsticked mouth, inhaled long and deep, dragoned smoke from her nose. She gazed out the window. At what? Her rose bushes? Her Mr. Lincolns and Orange Tropicanas?

The hummingbird feeder? The pear trees just beyond the split rail fence? "Alright then," she said to no one in particular. "Alright."

She must have heard Jimmer's stomach because she sliced a banana into two cereal bowls, one for me and one for Jimmer, sprinkled it with sugar and a splash of milk.

"To tide you over," she said, offering him the bowl and a spoon. She put her hand on his shoulder, gave it a squeeze, her fingers fluttered to Jimmer's brooch, which she had pinned to her blouse, and smiled. "Darling boy," she said. "What's to come of you?" Then sighed. "What's to come of all of us."

She didn't see him flinch, as if she had burned him with her touch, but I did. His face paled as Mom's grew rosy, the worry lines that crowded her forehead all but disappeared. He clenched his spoon, knuckles blanched. For just a moment he closed his eyes, took a deep breath. And then he was smiling again, eating his bananas and sugar milk.

That's the way it was with Jimmer. He felt everything. He was our mirror and emotional sponge. Our worries barnacled to his neck, and chest, and gut, the insides of his wrist. He seemed to understand what we needed at any given moment. He could fix things with the stuff inside him and the things he retrieved from his seemingly-bottomless duffle bag. We should have known that eventually it would all take its toll, that Jimmer would become a walking pressure cooker, ready to explode.

I especially should have known. But while Jimmer felt everything, I, after much practice, felt nothing at all.

We had to do all sorts of things to get the house ready for closing, spackling nail holes, touching up paint, washing baseboards and windowsills, caulking the space between the bathroom tiles and sink. We all pitched in, even my father, who unearthed his toolbox, fixed the hinges on the kitchen cabinets, tightened screws in the ceiling fixtures, moved the stove and the refrigerator so we could sweep out decades-old crumbs and cobwebs, mop up the kitchen grease and grime. For a moment my father gave us a glimpse of him giving a shit, renewing our hunger for something we couldn't articulate, a love and caring beyond our reach.

After a few pleasant days of what almost felt like normal, my father left again, allegedly to give the Atlantic states a go. He didn't know when he would return. With a reluctant sigh, he professed his apologies for failing to help with the move to the new place. He left a wad of cash and, of course, he left Jimmer.

Jimmer slept on the floor in a sleeping bag he pulled from his duffle. In the mornings, he walked me to school. The neighborhood kids, envious of my new big brother, skipped around us wanting to know where he'd come from. To the little ones, he claimed that he sailed from the deepest Peru just like Paddington and was found at a train station with a note pinned to his sleeve that said, *Please take good care of this bear.* "You're not a bear!" they chorused. "Are you sure?" he growled, and then confessed that, actually, he'd been found in the forest by an old witch, a tree fairy in disguise. It was the tree fairy who gifted him the very duffle bag he carried on his back and it was full of all sorts of magical things. He reached in and produced a handful of candies, red hots and Bazooka bubble gum, to share. To the older boys, as he rode around the neighborhood on a borrowed banana bike, he recounted adventures on motorcycles with Evil Knievel and Steve McQueen.

To Margot, after school, Jimmer regaled his life amongst the underground French aristocracy, his walks with poets in the Bois de Boulogne, the feasts of baguettes and fromage. Using Margot's eye-liner, they painted black mustachios on each other. With upturned noses and exaggerated accents, they teased me with their secrets as they threw French phrases round the room.

To me, late at night, Jimmer in his sleeping bag on my bedroom floor and me turned on my side in my single bed, he whispered up to me about the time he sailed over the mountains in a hot air balloon, the years he lived in a tree house in a redwood forest, the time he was a pearl diver in La Paz.

I knew of course, even then, that these stories were fabrications, and as much as I tried to pry it out of him, Jimmer's provenance remained a mystery. In the beginning, it didn't matter, at least not to me. But later I wondered. Did my father kidnap him? Was his mother in jail, dead, or had she simply disappeared? Were all his stories just a mask to hide the shame of being abandoned, unclaimed? Later, of course, it would all become very clear what Mom knew all along, what Margot suspected, what I blocked out as a kid, the wonderful mystery of him and the awful truth.

The apartment in Akron was actually a three-bedroom townhouse. Ours was the second one from the end, a gloomy tunnel with shared walls on either side, windows and daylight only at the ends. Cars whizzed by out front. Out back, from the kitchen window and the little balcony, we could see a ribbon of plain green lawn with no trees and more apartments and duplexes just beyond. Our new life was like stepping into *The Wizard of Oz* movie in reverse, vibrant technicolor fading into sepia-toned black and white.

Still, we tried to make a go of it and everything was pretty good for a while. As we settled in, that summer unfurled almost like an exotic vacation. We all got jobs and Mom, in particular, reveled in the feeling of getting paid for work for the first time. She started in the shoe department at O'Neill's and eventually worked her way up to furs and designer dresses. Margot pulled double shifts at Bob's Big Boy until she lied about her age and scored a gig as a cocktail waitress down in the Valley. Jimmer and I inherited a paper route from the kid who used to live in our place. Every morning at four fifteen, the *Akron Beacon Journal* truck dumped bundles of news and extras at the end of the driveway, which had to be assembled and delivered by six. I helped insert the entertainment section, the *Parade* magazine, the funnies and the advertisements, rubber banded the papers into logs. Jimmer packed his green duffle bag, and I packed the rest in a canvas tote provided by the *Journal*. I had never been up and out of the house so early in the morning. The neighborhood seemed less menacing in the chilly predawn hours, with few cars stirring, most of the houses still dark, the raucous chatter of the early birds and the distant whistle of a train. I didn't mind the weight of the papers, the pinch of canvas bag strap burrowing into my collar bone, as we worked our way through the maze of multifamily homes behind us, our efforts punctuated by the satisfying sound of the papers thwacking as Jimmer and I tossed them on doorsteps.

Back at our place, Mom was just waking up. Jimmer would make her toast with orange marmalade, just like Paddington, and instant coffee in her favorite teacup, the forget-me-not, one of the last pieces of the Royal Albert her grandmother brought over from England. "No one has ever waited on me like this before." Jimmer, what a darling boy.

Mom relied on Jimmer to keep an eye on me while she was at work, most days from ten in the morning until nine at night.

Jimmer and I kept the house tidy, laundered, and vacuumed. Jimmer made a game of it, making siren noises for the doomsday alarm that we set in the kitchen, a timer by which all chores had to be done. Then we were free to explore. Just a few blocks from Market Street, the main drag, as Mom would say, with paper route money in our pockets. We could walk carefully on the slim shoulder to the intersection of Market and Miller, to the bowling alley where we played pinball and the putt putt golf where Jimmer flirted with a girl name Janelle, and the movie theater which mostly played R-rated movies. To the west, we could walk to the mall and the library, and a pretty little cemetery. A walk to the east led to a dozen or so eateries, including Bob's and Rizzi's Pizza and Barnhill's Ye Old Fashioned Ice Cream Shoppe and best of all Skyway with its Sky High burgers on sweet buns, chocolate milk shakes, the grape ginger ale drink they called a California, and crispy onion rings.

On hot afternoons, we cranked up the AC even though we weren't supposed to because of the expense and watched TV, curled like puppies, heads on each other's rumps, watching reruns of *Lost in Space* and *Batman*, then *Match Game 74* and *Speed Racer*.

On the weekends, we watched cartoons, the *Wide World of Sports—the thrill of victory and the agony of defeat.* Every time I saw that ski jumper, I held my breath hoping this time he'd sail into the air instead of inevitably spinning out of control, skis crossed as he crashed.

We played Scrabble and Risk and gin rummy. Four-way solitaire when Mom and Margot were around.

I remember all the trouble started at the end of summer, when the carnival came to town, just before school started, when Margot began to disappear for real, when Mrs. Stevens moved in next door. But my memory fuses all the months and years together. They spin like whirligigs, like carnival rides, distorted like funhouse mirrors.

Back in those days, school started after Labor Day. And everyone had one last beautiful long weekend of summer with barbeques and pool parties. All the Pops in their aprons and long-handled spatulas flipping burgers and sipping beers. All the Paw Paws and Meemaws and elderly aunties shading in garages, sitting on green woven lawn chairs, occasionally getting up to scold the kids running in and out or to attend the food laid out on folding tables, the potato, macaroni and Jello salads, the baked beans, the celery sticks slicked with cream cheese and peanut butter, the deviled eggs. And later, as the day drew to a close, they'd all hop in their station wagons and attend the carnival set up in the vast parking lot at the mall.

Jimmer and I walked there, pockets full of paper route money and a little extra from Mom. Jimmer held my hand. I knew I was too old to skip but I did it anyway, intoxicated by the smell of cotton candy and popcorn, the calliope music spinning the merry-go-round, the rainbow of blinking lights on the Ferris wheel and the Tilt-a-Whirl, the mad riot of dodge-em cars, and the lure of games with darts and balloons, the chance of large stuffed teddy bears and plastic blow-up aliens which I begged Jimmer to win for me. Fortune tellers and acrobats dressed up like court jesters milled about.

And then there was the parade. Like none that I had ever seen before or since. Parents snatched their kids away and hissed with disgust as the horribles marched by. Instead of horses and elephants all dressed up in silks and feathers ridden by dazzling girls in sparkling leotards, there were men and woman with huge grotesque masks, parodies of politicians, Nixon and Spiro Agnew and the governor who sent National Guard troops to Kent State, sneering papier-mâché bobble heads, pulling carts of children in cages, old ladies in gas masks pushed in wheelchairs. They pelted us with salt water taffy as if we were a little New England town on the shore. One hunchback with an enormous hooked nose cackled then pointed at Jimmer. She reached out and grabbed his wrist. "Hey, Boy!" she said. Before he had a chance to fling her away, she said, "I've been looking for you ever since Topeka. Remember that thing you took? It's time to give it back." She clawed after him again, getting a hand hold on his duffle bag. It ripped, just a little, along the seam, as he wrestled it out of her crooked hands.

I looked up into Jimmer's face. I thought he'd be laughing, the joke of the crazy lady pretending to know him. Instead, he looked scared. "Come on Cissy," he said pushing me into the crowd. The hunchback yelled after us. "Freak!" she screamed. Her accusations splintered the night like fractals of carnival lights.

I started to cry as he dragged me past the games, the stuffed teddys and the green aliens, past the funnel cakes and corn dogs. I cried because Jimmer was scared, because of his unrelenting grip on my hand, because of the untapped possibilities of the fair. I wanted Jimmer to make it better, to tell me a story, how that witch had no power over Jimmer and therefore no power over me. But Jimmer refused to talk about what happened, even back at home when Mom found him slump shouldered in the front hall, examining the torn corner of his duffle, palming away his tears then wiping his nose across his sleeve. From her sewing kit, Mom produced a tapestry needle that could pierce the canvas with ease and some sturdy cotton thread, black was the best she could do. For her darling boy, she showed him how to fix the rip with a basket stitch. Jimmer took over the task, crisscrossing the frayed seam, over and over, until the hole was securely closed. "All better?" she said, examining his handiwork. Jimmer nodded yes and flashed his dimpled smile. But I could tell that Jimmer wasn't better at all, that a little bit of his magic had spilled out during the tussle at the parade, the confrontation tearing the fabric of a universe that, up until that point, Jimmer had managed to hold together. The black stitches embroidered a warning only Jimmer could decipher.

Jimmer turned fourteen, then fifteen, then sixteen, then seventeen. He grew and grew like a bean stalk, and we used most of our paper route money feeding his endless appetite, Sky High burgers, chocolate shakes, Italian fried chicken and jojos from Rizzi's. In one month alone he added two inches to his height, and started to smell; mom bought him deodorant and a shaving kit and removed him from my bedroom floor when I reported the funny tent pole Jimmer woke up with in the mornings. His teachers at the high school didn't like his cool cat attitude, wouldn't tolerate his restlessness, blurting out answers without raising his hand and getting the other kids all riled up. They didn't find his fairy tales charming. "More like smarting off if you ask me," the chemistry teacher said. They worried about what he was hiding in his green duffle bag back in the days when the worst they could imagine was weed and porno mags. Mom took off work to speak to the principal. "This is not my Jimmer, my darling boy." She wasn't going to drug her darling boy with Ritalin, but she would get his IQ tested. "Perhaps he's just bored at your damn school."

We used to sit at the top of the stairs listening to Mom sweet talking my father on the downstairs phone. Cooing then begging him to send money, to pay off the credit cards he'd run up, the gas and the electric. We could barely make ends meet. Jimmer needed private school and glasses. As an afterthought, she added, "and ballet lessons for Cissy, if we can swing it." Instead, he sent cases of the frozen fish slime, Tab, and rice cakes. Only Margot ate the diet food, the pounds began to melt away, and her once lovely curvaceous body was suddenly model thin. She quit college, stopped wearing a bra and took up with Roy who lived out in Hinckley next to the lake where the buzzards came to roost.

On nights Margot didn't come home, Mom packed Jimmer and me into her green Satellite Sebring, drove twenty minutes in the dead of night, sent Jimmer to rap on Roy's cedar wood door. Sometimes, Roy answered in his wife beater, a beer in his hand, laughing that they'd lost track of time. He produced a disheveled Margot, all apologies. Margot, flushed and happy, with a hickey on her neck, willingly left Roy's doorstep and came along with us. Other nights, well other nights were a different story. When Roy wouldn't answer the knock on the door. When Jimmer couldn't persuade Margot *to just fucking get into the car*. When Margot screamed at Mom for ruining her life.

This was about the time Margot threw out the box she never unpacked, the one labeled Margot's Hall of Fame, and when Jimmer started cutting himself. I watched from the shadows in the hallway, the two of them sitting on the bathroom floor. "Let me do it for you," he said. He gently pried a razor blade from her hand, held it up to the light, then Jimmer pressed the blade into his own flesh, on his forearm, just below his elbow crease. Together they watched the blood pearl. Margot cried about all of her lost potential, how her best laid plans had gone awry. Jimmer handed her a wad of toilet paper to blow her nose, another wad to dab at the eyeliner streaking her cheeks. She laid her head on Jimmer's shoulder. While Jimmer bled, Margot fell asleep.

Mom always blamed herself for getting him the shaving kit, with twenty single-edge razor blades. But I knew he would have found something else to relieve Margot's pain, perhaps a safety pin or the Swiss Army knife he kept in the side pocket of his duffle.

The next time my father showed up, he brought Mrs. Stevens, a twenty-eight-year-old "widow" he installed in the townhouse next to ours. She came with a baby grand piano, a Persian cat, expensive taste, and a desire for culture. She and my father played house for a while. It was weird when she invited us over for dinner to show off her snazzy recipes that were decidedly not diet food: chicken cordon bleu, corn souffle, crepe Suzette, and chocolate fondue. My father got snazzy too. Leisure suits and paisley shirts with wide pointy collars, white patent leather shoes. He grew his sideburns long. When he took Mrs. Stevens out to the Agora, they were chased by crazed fans who mistook him for that guy who sang "What's new pussycat? Whoa, whoa, whoa."

Mom ignored the spectacle the best she could. She knew he would soon get bored. When my father left again, this time for the South and then cowboy territory, Texas and Oklahoma, New Mexico, Mrs. Stevens, face bloated from crying, false eyelashes dangling like unhinged spiders from her eyes, sought my mother's counsel. All out of tears, I heard Mrs. Steven's loud laugh that emanated from deep down in her belly. "When Cliff convinced me to quit my concert tour, he said he would take care of me. Now what the fuck am I supposed to do?" Mrs. Stevens said. Mom took a long drag of her cigarette. She knew what it was like to quit a career before it ever really got started, the law school plans that got shelved along with debate team trophies, the tarnished key to the city she had been given when she won the national VFW essay contest, all that prize money she used as a down payment on the house back in Hudson. Coolly, she said, "Get a job. I hear there's an opening down at Riviera Lanes. It's down at the corner of Market and Miller." And because Jimmer needed something better to do with his hands, Mom swallowed her pride and asked Mrs. Stevens to introduce Jimmer to her piano. It was Mrs. Stevens who taught Jimmer the Gershwin song. Through the thin walls that separated our place from hers, we could hear the keys, the slow build— the flirtatious trill, playful, dancey and then maniacal.

My father had made Mom and Mrs. Stevens enemies. Their love for Jimmer, their darling boy, created an uneasy alliance. Jimmer didn't get his private school, but he got private tutelage of another kind from Mrs. Stevens: the piano of course and art museums and lectures and when they went to the symphony, with Jimmer on her arm, Mrs. Stevens would dress up in a red evening gown, pulling on long opera gloves, and pretend she was going to the Metropolitan Opera House instead of the Akron Civic Center. I never did get my ballet lessons.

Mrs. Stevens joined us on our weekly trips to tug Margot away from Roy's lair. Until one day we found an orange eviction notice, all of Roy's shit on the stoop. No Roy. No Margot. Just Margot's makeup bag which Jimmer snatched and stuffed into his duffle bag.

When Jimmer wasn't playing the piano or escorting Mrs. Stevens, he was up in Mom's room, sitting on the edge of her bed, the two of them smoking cigarettes and reading passages from *The Bell Jar*, a tattered used version that he found tucked in the furthest corner of his bag. Mom and Jimmer channeling Sylvia Plath, reminding each other to keep on living, as they recited, sometimes in unison: *"I took a deep breath and listened to the old brag of my heart. I am, I am, I am."* After Margot disappeared for real, Mom only wanted Jimmer. Jimmer soaked up all of her misery. He brought her aspirin and cold compresses, and an occasional Irish cream in the forget-me-not cup.

Meanwhile, I became invisible, sometimes crawling into Jimmer's green duffle bag, next to his tube socks and magic tricks, zipping myself in. I wondered if Jimmer would find me in there, use me up. For something good or for something bad, I didn't care which.

I lost myself in school and the track team in which I was the only girl, running round and round the junior high's makeshift track, a circular asphalt driveway dotted with potholes and dandelions growing through the cracks. I lost myself in the ache of my budding breasts, the new and peculiar sensations between my legs, and the stack of gothic romances I brought home from the library each week. It felt like I was living in one of those books, in a crumbling estate, with Margot's ghost haunting me at every turn, Mom and Mrs. Stevens scratching at the wallpaper, Jimmer a benign version of Heathcliff.

When my father went on a bender, lost his job and his latest stewardess/nurse/playboy-bunny girlfriend, he crawled back to the townhouses on Miller Road hoping to bunk in with either Mom or Mrs. Stevens. Jimmer confronted him, told him that neither woman would have him. My father, furious, accused us all of being parasites and Jimmer was "nothing more than a little bastard trying get a piece of ass from the likes of that whore Mrs. Stevens."

"Fuck you, man. You ruin everything!" Jimmer said.

It would have made sense that the climax of the whole ugly parade of horribles, not the one at the carnival, rather the one that had become my life, would have happened right then and there. But it was months later, just a few days before the freshman formal. My beautiful white eyelet dress that I had bought with paper route money, hanging in the closet, a pair of cork-soled, strappy white platform sandals centered underneath.

I'm not really sure how or why it happened. By that time, Mrs. Stevens and her Persian cat and her baby grand piano had moved in with us. The place was cluttered with people and things, cat hair and fur balls, the smell of litter box, Mrs. Steven's belly laugh and Jimmer's manic rhapsodic pounding on those Steinway keys. There was no retreat, no way to package up my feelings and stick them in a box. I couldn't smile and forget all the bad stuff like I usually did. It seeped into my skin, underneath my fingernails, the follicles out of which my voluminous hair grew.

I was mouthing off I suppose. I was sick and tired of Jimmer telling me what to do. I didn't want, just this one time, to take Mom her coffee, and maybe clean up the kitchen too. There were large black ants hiding under the dirty dishes piling up in the sink, scurrying underneath last night's skillet of fried eggs, last week's pot of chili.

"Come on, Cissy. Mom does all these great things for you. I can't do it because I have this piano recital thing with Mrs. Stevens I've got to get ready for."

"Don't call her mom. She's not *your* mom. She's *my* mom. Go be with Mrs. Stevens, if you must. She could be your mom, or is she like your girlfriend now?"

"Shut up."

"That's what I heard Dad say, that's why he got so mad, you made him leave again."

"Shut up, shut up, shut up."

I don't know what finally made Jimmer snap like a taut rubber band, like the ones on the Sunday paper logs we delivered, stretched beyond capacity.

But when it happened, it changed my life forever, because everyone chose Jimmer: Mom, Mrs. Stevens, Margot's ghost. Even I chose Jimmer. Because after all, I was just quiet, invisible Cissy. He was our darling boy, Jimmer. In my head, I always accuse my father, already rotten and fallible. It's his fist I see when I look in the mirror. There's no use getting into the details because my mind can't summon them, there's only before and after.

The eye patch was Jimmer's idea. The one he gifted me from his green duffle bag when he first arrived. He cried when he stretched the elastic band over my head, smoothed the tangles of my frizzy hair and then gently settled the fabric over the swollen rose bud of my eye, purple and ready to bloom. I was surprised by the weight of the flimsy piece of flannel. It would be weeks before the surgeon could cut me open, access the broken bones, wire them together, then Picasso my nose and cheek back into an approximation of the former real estate of my face. Then weeks more for the swelling to go down.

Jimmer tried to make things right. "My god, you can't go to the ninth-grade dance looking like that!" He wanted to erase everything that happened and I wanted to allow him his moment. He cradled my face with his beautiful hands, hands that should have been waltzing across ivory keys. They were cool, smelled like soap, soothed the ache that was growing in my jaw and face. He kissed the top of my head. He stood back to assess his handiwork.

"This could work." He circled around me. He did that corny thing where a director holds up his hands as if they're a movie screen, like he can picture the drama spinning in his head. He made up my story. "Channel your inner pirate!" he said. "I can see it now. You're a swashbuckling Cinderella who just vanquished a whale."

Margot's ghost quickly nixed the idea because the bruise swelled beyond the oval of the patch. And besides, she said, "Cissy's not the swashbuckling type."

Little sisters don't have adventures. They're little pets or potted plants, part of the scenery, the décor, like a vase inconveniently in the way, in the middle of a dispute, collateral damage from friendly fire.

Jimmer fetched Margot's makeup bag, used her easy, breezy, beautiful, CoverGirl to camouflage the damage, brushed the foundation on liberally, I winced with each brush stroke and Margot commanded me to sit still.

Mrs. Stevens joined in, grabbed the mascara and then sighed, a little put out by the effort it would take to mask me into something presentable. "You have no eyelashes—what have you been doing? pulling them out?"

She used the eyeliner to raccoon the other eye, flourished swipes of blue and pink eye shadow to see if she could make them match, but she couldn't CoverGirl me beautiful.

"Don't be ridiculous," Mom said from the doorway, a cigarette dangling from her mouth. She held up scissors and gauze and surgical tape. In an effort to hide the evidence, they snipped and ripped and plastered strips of gauze across my eye and the offending bruises, making me into a comic book villain, the half-faced mummy.

We all looked in the old mirror, crazing at the edges, the one that had cracked in the melee. We stared at the reflection of us, a vintage framed portrait of our weird makeshift family, Mom, Margot's ghost, Jimmer, Mrs. Stevens and me. We were all broken beyond repair.

Mom drove me and my reluctant date to the dance. The principal who was manning the entrance pulled her aside. "I'm really supposed to report this sort of thing, Victoria." But Mom convinced him that there was nothing to report at all. He nodded agreeably, happy to wash his hands of any responsibility. And so, I paraded into the dance in my white eyelet dress and high heels, the phantom of the opera, a monstrous one-eyed cyclops. I did not wallflower myself on the sidelines or hide underneath the bleachers. I discoed under the fractured mirror ball light. I was no longer invisible.

WHEN THE OLD GANG GETS TOGETHER, they clamor to tell the legend, the only one they know. Picture a civilized brawl of laughter, of smoke, everyone chawing over one another, getting louder and louder with their embellishments. Swigging their beers. Shuffling a deck of cards with a satisfying and extended thwack. Dealing clubs and spades, aces, and jacks. Deep in someone's basement hideaway with a rumble of weekend kids galloping up above, high on Halloween leftovers: Almond Joys and Sugar Daddys, semi-thawed from forgotten pockets of the deep freeze, like everyone's collective memory, stale with the lingering taste of nostalgia and frost-bitten deer meat.

There's Big Dave and Skunk, Trevor, my brother Eddie and me, that dude from Findlay who always wears his Marathon Oil trucker hat and a few other guys who cycle in and out. Below ground it's the 80s. Everyone is beautiful in their sockless topsiders, striped rugby shirts, and popped up collars. Wide-grinned and Ray-Banned, dreaming of their Firebirds and Camaros, bright shiny futures primed for endless opportunities, and a collective amnesia for all their youthful indiscretions. Above ground, everyone is paunchy, hairlines receding to counter their expanding girths and wallets, their sprawling Tudors on East River Road, fortressed with stone walls and gated entrances that look like gaping toothy maws.

And then there's me. Above and below, I'm Eddie's younger brother, a rattle of bones, rarely sober, occasionally solvent, forgettable really except for Dog curled companionably at my feet and the book I wrote that everyone heard was important but never bothered to read.

Below ground everyone sorts their cards into little fans, holds them close to the vest. They toss out tales like poker chips, upping the ante. Plink after plink after plink.

"Remember her?" everyone says. "That crazy-haired chick from the outskirts of campus, beyond the railroad tracks, the grain elevators and the fallow fields? The one who was so randy no one could believe the shit she'd do?" Plink. "Hell yeah," they say with a deep throated chuckle, "that white-trash witch-girl with a masters in biology or forestry or something, already working on a PhD." Plink. "Remember the night the fraternity pledges disappeared?" The Kappa Sigs were having a tea. She virgined her way in, danced at their party, ping ponged their red cups, and if you can believe it, Pied Pipered them out the door, across campus, past the ice rink and the football stadium, all the way to the abandoned farmhouse, where, with some sort of sexy trickery, she voodooed their souls. Plink, plink, plink, plink, plink.

Everyone shudders at the thought of her body, with all of its luscious curves, hidden underneath the prim folds of her Laura Ashley calicos, the acuity of her mind, her facility with numbers and facts and formulas, her promise that just a little tutoring could yield all the right answers on their quantum physics exam. What it must have felt like to be with her just before she dumped them into a bog somewhere out on Devil's Hole Road. She didn't even say thank you. The poor bastards didn't stand a chance.

I remember, but keep to myself, visions of her camped out beyond the farmhouse in the windbreak next to Hazel's Pond, amidst the scrubby pines, the laurel bushes, the swamp oak and the ash trees. How she decorated their branches with her lacy lavender bras and the clatter of cooking utensils, little shovels and trowels and specimen vials. How she ate caterpillars and aphids and sucked dew from leaves. The shape of her heart-shaped ass as she bathed in the aching shimmer of the moon. How much she fucking loved those trees.

Her name was Cassandra, Cassie for short, although she'd change it randomly and without explanation calling herself Beatrice or Phoebe or Liza or a half-dozen other names claiming she'd always been known as such. And while I was sure that I'd met her before she denied that too. But then she'd lean in, her warm breath sweet as honeysuckle, and whisper, "Yes, I think we have met before, when you were a better version of yourself, when you were just a boy."

The first time (or perhaps the second time) I saw Cassie, she was walking barefoot across the commons towards the library, her arms bursting with books, reddish cloth-bound pomegranates, borrowed from the antiquarian archives. She was tall, and her limbs so thin she reminded me of a sapling, newly planted, tender and fragile, bending in the wind. Her hair sparked out in every direction, a thick root ball of threadlike filaments that frizzed about her head like a halo. The ends twitched, not quite like Medusa's snakes but mesmerizing nonetheless.

I followed her into the building, up the elevator to the eighth floor, hung out in the stacks just outside the door of her grad student cubby, then on to the Admin Building—to what was supposed to be the top-secret location of the university's human intelligence office, also known as Fact Line, the eighties telephone version of Google. From there, I trailed her to wherever she was living at the time, nowhere and everywhere, the library, the abandoned farmhouse, underneath an old oak tree. I wish I could say it was love, but like those pledges, I was driven by my need.

Ω

The gang discards their castoffs, hoping for something better the second time around. From a scratchy LP on a refurbished turntable, Pat Benatar sings.

As they draw new cards, everyone remembers how the pledges reemerged, one by one, quiet and sullen, dragging their feet, resentful because they had been promised the secrets of the universe. In the root cellar, round back of the old farmhouse, they did as they were told. They navigated the rickety stairs, the cobwebs, the mason jars of pickled god-knows-what, the frightening piles of potatoes, carrots, turnips, and beets. The rock-hard dirt floor. How she offered up a burlap sack to place underneath their heads and commanded them to look for the nineteenth step (or the eighteenth, depending on who you ask) as she closed the doors and locked them in. They saw nothing, the damn fools, nothing but their own withering pricks.

Ω

When Cassie finally gave me her number, she scribbled it on a scrap of paper torn from one of her pomegranate books. It took me a few days, but when I dialed it, some dude answered, "Yo." I was crestfallen and angry until I heard, "This is Fact Line. What's your question?"

I first heard about Fact Line from Big Dave, my RA back then, who refused to demean himself by posturing as anything other than the massive lout at the end of the hallway, who looked like he should be playing the tuba rather than the piccolo in the university marching band. The position of resident advisor merely a way to reduce his fees, he had no interest, as he said, in being a babysitter, nursemaid, or mother. He called a meeting the first night we moved in, handed us each a ribbon of condoms and a slip of paper and said, "This is the only advice you'll ever get from me. Ask permission and use protection. Beyond that—call this number for Fact Line. Everything you need to know, everything you'll ever want to know, at the touch of your fingertips. Otherwise, fuck off." He would turn up again later in my brother's law firm, larger than ever, a big swaggering dick.

I didn't know whether to hang up or to ask any number of inane questions I had heard the guys in the hall ask like: When is Thanksgiving break, what are the drink specials at Howards, do fish get seasick, what are the hockey scores, what rhymes with orange, what's the number for Myles pizza pub, how tall is a Smurf, who shot JR, what exactly is 3-2 beer, how many licks does it take to get to the center of a Tootsie Pop, where's the sexy legs contest, what's the best cure for a cold, heartbreak, or hangover, do those over-the-counter pregnancy tests really work, do girls really just wanna have fun?

As I contemplated the possibilities, the dude huffed beyond the receiver. "It's one of those heavy breathers," he said. "It's for Cassie." From across the void, which I envisioned to be a room full of pencil-necked geeks, I heard: "Cassie's not here. Tell whoever, him or her, to call back."

That night and every night, for what felt like weeks, I called again and again, suffering through busy signals, becoming more desperate with each missed connection until Cassie finally answered, "Fact Line, what's your question?"

She had this way, even over the phone, to stun me into silence.

"Is it you?" she said. Her voice tinny and crackling, obscured by the frayed telephone lines swaying in the corn fields, plagued by perching crows and thunderstorms.

"Yes. I mean no. Maybe?" My voice cracked and the lump in my throat got stuck like I'd just swallowed peanut butter on a cracker. It was embarrassing but I blubbered on. "I don't really know who I am. I mean how do you grow into a person without a mother? Mine died when I was ten and so did my father. My brother, my half-brother, his name is Eddie, hates me because he thinks my mother, his stepmother, was the one driving the car. You know what he called me yesterday when I called and asked for a small loan to buy books? He said I was nothing, a parasite, a fucking amoeba. And that I had no future. Could that be true? I mean amoebas don't even fuck, right?"

"Amoebas reproduce asexually. But that's not really your question is it? You want to know who you are, how you fit into this time and place. And where people go when they die, right?"

I was confused.

"Time is just a social construct," Cassie said. "There is no past, present, or future. Time meanders around like a maze, a labyrinth. It bends and curves, and divides into forking paths, into multiple, parallel universes, like a library full of books. And in one of those, or maybe many more, your mother is very much alive. And in some, *you* don't even exist."

"I don't think this is helping," I sputtered. "In some universes I don't exist?"

"You're on the track team, right? Do you ever wonder why you run in that little circle around the track, running faster and faster but never getting anywhere? It feels like you're going nowhere in that loop but actually you are going everywhere, working out every possibility."

I was more confused than ever. I told her that Fact Line was a crock of shit.

"Look, some questions are easy to answer, a factoid anyone can understand. The big answers require big questions from great thinkers. What will it be, Rusty? You ready to question? Ready to think? Are you ready for conundrums, geometrical ponderings, radical enlightenment?"

She kept on like that, asking me questions. She knew what I wanted. My thirst was so great. I imagined her reaching past the phone books, the Farmer's Almanac and atlas, periodic tables, a Roget's thesaurus, encyclopedias (Britannica and the World Book), the university handbook, binders of compiled class catalogues and schedules, index cards taped to the wall with event locations, sports scores, concert times, driving directions, and movie times.

She read to me, for hours, from the red books I'd mistaken for pomegranates and ancient texts, the handwritten draft of her dissertation, her epic poem, the history of the universe.

Ω

Everyone places their bets. Amidst the cigar smoke, they call or raise. With the stakes so high, Skunk and Trevor and the Marathon man, each in turn say I'm out.

"What about you, brother?" Eddie smirks. "Are you ready to fold?"

Ω

Cassie had been sleeping in my bed for three weeks when things started getting weird. Her long legs and her pomegranates took up the entirety of my single XL. I sat at her feet, relegated to the floor and pressed into service as her errand boy. She had been evicted from her eighth-floor cubby when the staff discovered she'd been spending her nights there. The other places, likewise, would not accommodate her at the moment. She'd needed a place that was warm and dry, with electric lights. This was no time to be charming with candlelight. She was in the throes of finishing her epic poem. She sat in my bed, scribbling incessantly, her hair in a dazzling state of perpetual bedhead, split ends twitching like exclamation points to the frantic sweep of hands across the paper. At night she wiggled out of her prairie dress and slept in my buffalo plaid.

She'd go for hours without eating and then suddenly declare, "I need sustenance! I'm famished! I'm absolutely starving!" Using my coupon books, I'd buy her food from the cafeteria and bring it up on a tray. She'd dawdle over her cobb salad, occasionally snitching one or two of my fries. Later, on my way back from class, I'd find her clawing in a flower bed, stuffing clods of dirt and moss into her mouth.

In the mornings, just before sunrise, she'd walk into the woods, before forest bathing was a thing. She said she needed to recharge, to get answers, to visit her oak tree. From my window, I'd watch her leave me, a phantom in her peasant dress, my plaid shirt for a jacket, her feet encumbered in a pair of my old work boots.

I missed our late-night phone calls. Now that she was living in my room, inches away from the black rotary phone where it all began, she hardly spoke to me at all. I became moody and sullen. I began to whine.

"What is it, Rusty?" She sighed in that way that I knew I was pushing myself right out of her life, just when I'd gotten used to fetching her tampons and what-nots, filling little sandwich baggies full of dirt, which she stashed under her (my) pillow, in her book bag, in the pockets of my shirt. We were drinking lime rickeys and the gin buzzed my nerves. I grimaced from its cloying sweetness, from the simple syrup she made in my plug-in hot pot and the weird taste of her homemade tonic.

"We never talk anymore," I said.

She pushed aside her pomegranates and patted the bed. Gratefully, I sat next to her.

"Tell me something, Rusty. What makes you special? What makes you, you?"

No one, including myself, ever thought I was special. I was the family fuck up, the loser who weaseled his way into college on track scholarship. She nudged me with her knee. Bone on bone. I peered into her eyes, such a cliché but really, I did it, I looked into Cassie's green eyes, searching for the right answer. "Do you mean can I do circus tricks? Walk on my hands, twist a cherry stem with my tongue?" I paused, waiting for confirmation. Receiving none, I filled the silent void, "Well, I can run a four-and-a-half-minute mile, I'm a Kappa Sig, I'm an orphan."

"Nope. That's not it," she said shaking her head. She pressed her pointer finger into my chest, jabbing harder with each assertion. "You're an empty vessel, a blank slate, ready to be written on, aching to be filled up. *That's* what you makes you special."

I was not sure how I felt about her saying all that, even though, in principle, I agreed. I wanted all that she could teach me, all that she held in the infinite maze that was her mind. For a moment I was hostile. This was not the kind of talking I was pining for. Where was the poetry, the Kant and Diderot, Simone de Beauvoir and Baruch Spinoza, Hélène Cixous? "What about you, what makes *you* so special?" I reached over to jab her in return but she swatted my hand away.

"Me?" she said straightening her spine. "I'm passionate. I've got goals. I'm chronicling, in verse, the entire history of the universe, from the beginning until the end of time, the future, the whole sordid mess of it all, everything I've learned from talking to the trees."

I laughed. Because what else can you do when you suddenly realize that your girlfriend is batshit crazy?

Ω

Underground, it's hazy from the cigar smoke and the bullshit. There's the constant racket of kids stomping down the stairs with bruises and bloody noses and belly aches from too much candy. The gang wonders briefly if they should have hired a babysitter or wrangled a first-year associate to supervise the upstairs—the progeny from their second and third wives.

I don't have any children, as far as anyone knows, and I watch with amusement as they inartfully comfort the little rugrats with a looksee at the offending wound, a pat on the back, and sometimes a tipple of beer before sending them back up to daylight.

And then, like a cartoon lightbulb over their heads, everyone suddenly turns to me and says, Rusty, you dated her, right?

Big Dave scratches his chin. "Wasn't that around the time your book came out. Just before she disappeared?"

Eddie is waiting. He doesn't care about the girl. "Are you going to fold or not?" he says.

I arrange my face into an inscrutable plain, a look I've practiced over the years. Another thing that pisses Eddie off. Eddie has never forgiven me for my unlikely success. Losing even one hand of poker to me is more than he can tolerate. There's never been a spotlight he's been willing to share.

Ω

My sullenness was soon replaced with Cassie's anger. One afternoon, she threw her pomegranates, one by one, against my dorm room wall. Forgetting, as I usually did, that they were books, not exotic fruits, I expected a thunderous splat with juice and seeds staining the walls. She raged against the administration, the college machine, the patriarchy, the committee who wouldn't sign off on her dissertation, wouldn't allow her, through the auspices of the university, to warn the world of the shit she'd come to know. They said her work was blather, the hysterical musings of an unserious mind. "Can you imagine, Rusty? Me an unserious mind?" she said.

We both knew what that meant. She didn't have to say it. She was a woman, no, just a girl.

Then came the nightmares. She'd wake up crying about orange circles painted on tree trunks. She pressed her hands against her head, her mop of hair quivered. "Can't you hear them?" she said. "The trees are screaming. The harvesters are coming. The earth is dying. And so am I."

I didn't know how to comfort her, so I rubbed her cold feet. My thumbs found Cassie's heartbeat in the halfmoon of her arches. She was very much alive.

Two nights later, Cassie led me across the campus, past the ice rink and the football field to the abandoned farmhouse, to the root cellar round back. She heaved opened the wooden doors. We descended into the darkness, pushing away cobwebs. The smell of earth and dead things rose up to greet us.

"I thought you should know. This is where I took the other boys. But they were just a dress rehearsal. I was trying them on. They were not you. They were not the right receptacle."

And then she led me to the thicket where I had followed her so long before, to the great swamp oak, no longer adorned with her things. Indeed, the rivulets of bark were stained orange with the forester's mark. They were slated for destruction.

Cassie laid down on her back underneath the tree, a pillow of rotting leaves cushioning her head. I was astonished to see the tumbleweed of her hair flatten and stretch out in every direction. Like yawning tentacles, her hair entwined with the swamp oak's roots which in turn connected to the roots of the river birch and the sugar maple and the sycamore tree. She smiled and told me she could hear the fungi crackle, the network of lacy mycorrhizae, centuries-old, spread out for miles and miles, whispering veiled secrets, the language of the trees. Arms outstretched, she'd beckoned me. "Come here, Rusty. You may think you chose me, but I chose you."

In my dorm room, she insisted on being on top. Out in the woods, it was different. For reasons I did not understand at the time, she delighted in suffering the hard cracked earth, the jab and pinch of rocks and sticks, the biting of ants and thorny things. And because I wanted to know all of her, all that she saw but could not convey in words, I did as I was told. I melted into her, under the canopy of the tree, rocking back and forth like a fishing boat on the choppy waves of Lake Erie, until her mouth formed what should have been a perfect "O" but resembled instead the wavy smirk of a clam shell.

And then....

And then, this is where my confession, if I were to give one, becomes difficult to articulate. This connection, this triumvirate, the girl, the tree, and me. It's a complicated equation.

Neither before nor since have I seen, with such clarity, the truth. With our tripling came: static electricity, sharp prickles and tiny white explosions and then for a moment nothing—like the world was holding its breath and then exhaled white noise like TV static back in the day when the TV slept—cut off from the world sometime around two AM—dozing off to the national anthem and a waving picture of the flag, until a hive of gray and black took over, leaving the night alone with its unspeakable sadness. And then I was swirling into a deep dark hole, pulled in by a powerful centrifugal force, it kaleidoscoped into bursting colors of orange and pink and cherry. I saw everything at once, an infinite history.

I saw the world broken open, cracked like an egg, its yolk and haloed effluvium spilled out onto the barren earth, filling its craters, becoming saltwater oceans and freshwater lakes, rivers and swamps. I saw the yolk burble and erupt, Mt. Vesuvius, spewing ash, pumice, sulfuric gas. I saw the ferny skeletons of rainbow trout, the curved spine of a fetus sucking its thumb. I saw an umbilical cord and its throbbing placenta spread and become a giant underground fungus, mushrooms born at the base of trees. I saw a round cluster of eggs, frogspawn dotted with tiny black dots, tadpoles emerging from jelly-filled sacs, a jet stream of sperm-like swimmers that bloomed into women. I saw sandy loam. I saw teeming fields of corn, endless stalks, green then yellowish-brown waving, whispering, rustling like plantation crinolines. I saw windows, reflections of me, looking at me, infinite me, tunnel of me. I saw that gothic mansion on Robinwood Drive, the one built by the Licorice King and later inhabited by an order of priests, Oblate Fathers heads bowed during evening vespers, the sway of the thurible, clouds of incense and smoke delivering their supplications, I saw their dread and uncertainty. I saw molten glass, hand-blown into a bulbous monstrosity, which divided and multiplied, again and again, until it formed into a behemoth thirty stories high. I saw tugboats and flats of coal. I saw a farmhand swallowed by grain. I saw a suited man sporting a bowler hat, encumbered with a tail and four legs—two human, two cloven. A book. Borges' first English edition of *The Aleph* translated by Norman Thomas Di Giovanni. I saw the wooly salamander, asbestos, a magic stone's long fibrous crystals that look like a frozen waterfall woven into indestructible, nonflammable cloth. I saw words on a page advising against the investment of quarry slaves. I saw hundreds, no thousands of screaming trees, girdled suffocated, asphyxiated, cut off at the wind pipes, left to die, felled, chopped, cannibalized, glorious trees brutalized, made into barrels, burned. Tears of sap. I saw melting ice caps, shifting magnetic poles, algae blooms. I saw the future and the horror of it took my breath away.

Ω

Like Eddie, everyone thinks they know me. I am the token man of letters. Benign. Still lean and lanky and bony-kneed from my spartan appetite and endless miles of running. A humble scarecrow in Dorothy's cornfield. I'm that guy, the underachiever who came out of nowhere. A literary genius, who produced, in a manic surge of inspiration, a magnum opus at the tender age of twenty. A twelve-hundred-page compendium of postmodern wisdoms and futurisms. *Publisher's Weekly* called *Unquenchable, The Thirst for Knowledge*, a triumph. *Newsweek* called me a hack and accused me of being an Alvin Toffler wannabe. *The Atlantic* compared me to a modern-day Pliny the Elder, Roman chronicler of all the known facts of the ancient world, snuffed out by a volcano in Pompeii, important only to philologists and asbestos attorneys. *Time* smugly dismissed me as a preposterous doomsayer threading ancient history with conspiracy theories and scientific hysteria predicting global warming, vanishing glaciers, giant algae blooms, and the fall of democracy.

Everyone remembers the time I met Phil Donahue and Sally Jessy Raphael. The lecture circuit and the honorary degrees. The toothpaste and Gatorade endorsements. And the patent infringement case for a new kind of polygraph machine—and this is where everyone snorts, pounding their fists to emphasize their laughter. Imagine: lies measured by the quivers of a spider plant, and a *tradescantia fluminensis variegata*.

Everyone wonders what I'm going to do next. It's been thirty years. My BMW, the one I bought from the proceeds of the book, is vintage now. The steps to my front porch are sagging. The twisting green vines of the Waverly wallpaper the interior decorator insisted upon should have been scraped off a decade ago. With a dwindling bank account, I have monetized my graying professorial charms. I have an office at the university. I teach a senior seminar. I ride a bicycle to campus. Dog sits in the wicker basket attached to the handlebars, his white cotton candy fur breezing as I pedal. I still have a full head of hair, thick and wavy in a handsome shade that matches Dog's. I've adopted a sculpted beard, a van dyke, to camouflage my weak chin.

And somehow, I've become a legend too. When some new environmental horror is uncovered, radioactive frogs, or two-headed calves, melting of artic glaciers, or tornados in December, I'm invited to make an appearance on CNN, or Terry Gross on Fresh Air reads an excerpt from my book and then gravels an incredulous "How did you know?"

Everyone, a chorus, fists pounding, feet stomping, echoes, "How did you know? How did you know?"

My shrugging shoulders, my dismissive grin. How do I explain the source of all that I know—all that I am and have become —all that I will never be again?

I've got nothing in my hand but I do not fold. I call and push the rest of my chips into the center of the table. Big Dave taps the table twice, "I'm out." Eddie throws his cards at me. "Lucky sonofabitch," he says. I survey my bounty. I gather my chips.

Acknowledgments

I AM GRATEFUL TO THE EDITORS of the following publications in which portions of this book first appeared, sometimes in slightly different versions.

"Legend" in *Iron Horse Literary Review*, Issue 27.1 (February 2025)

"Bird with Lavender Tongue" in *Prism International* Issue 60.1, Wonder (Fall 2021);

"Devil's Hole Road" in *Storm Cellar*, Issue 9.2, Fusion (Summer/Fall 2021); and

"The Esquire Ball," in *Meat for Tea,* Volume 15, Issue 1, Chuck (Spring 2020).

Deepest thanks to Diane Goettel, executive editor of Black Lawrence Press for saying yes to this book and the entire BLP team especially Angela Leroux-Lindsey for her close reading and insightful edits and Zoe Norvell for *Esquire Ball'*s enchanting cover design.

Many thanks to Ukrainian artist, Kateryna Repa for providing "Frog Painting" which captures the heart and soul of everything I'm trying to convey in this collection. And thank you the talented and generous Jacquelyn Cynkar who captured my heart and soul in my author photo. And to Will Amato for making it all come alive on my website.

This book would not be possible without the input, support and encouragement from many people over the course of the ten years it took me to write this book:

I'm forever indebted to the amazing group of women who comprise the Quaker Lake Writers: you and your work inspire me, and your companionship is essential, especially for Milena Nigam for gathering us together, your leadership and your kind hospitality each year. I'm grateful for the incomparable Sherrie Flick, wise teacher, thesis advisor, mentor and friend who believed in this collection from the very start. Sharla Yates, my best mate, who has been whispering the secrets of storytelling in my ear ever since our very first MFA class together. Thank you to Hallie Pritts and Stephanie Vega for the generosity of your time, insightful critiques and cheers for every positive rejection. Thank you to Bergita Bugarija for pushing me to find the heart of every story and for your boundless energy and contagious enthusiasm.

Thank you to my Chatham University MFA family—professors, visiting faculty and peers especially Sherrie Flick, Marc Nieson, Sheila Squillante, Robert Yune, Paul Hertneky, Tim Parrish, Christopher Barzak, and Stuart Hunt, the beautiful soul who left us too soon.

Thank you to my other teachers I've met along the way whose body of work, kind words, editorial and publishing opportunities and insight helped me find my voice: Margot Livesey, Laura Van den Berg, Ann Pancake, Louis Alberto Urrea, Christopher Chambers, John Mauk, Clare Beams, Anjali Sachdeva, Danielle Chiotti, Peg Alford Pursell, Christine Stroud, and Brittany Hailer and her nana.

Thank you to my SCBWI Peters Township writing group who helped me eke out my first tentative sentences and paragraphs: Sabrina (just get it done) Fedel, Cristina Rouvalis, Amanda Hooper, Stephanie Logue, Tom Atkins and our fearless leader Pat Easton.

I'm so grateful for my brilliant Canadian friends, Justice Sandra Antoniani and Justice Gina Papageorgiou, who helped me navigate my early days as an expat lawyer on Bay Street and beyond and who have stood by me and my various iterations as a human.

Thank you to my dear friend Tina Brinsky for all the miles of running and walking during which you listened to me explain the early versions of these stories, and for never forgetting a detail.

Thank you to my family who never gave up on me despite the endless number of years the idea of writing a book had been percolating. My sister Candace Logan, the bravest and strongest person I know who told me not to despair, that everyone has a different timeline, so just keep moving forward on mine. My mother, Thalia Hergenroeder Slage, who inspired us with her stories of winning the VFW national essay contest on patriotism, the mayor's proclamation of Thalia Day, and the parade held in her honor after which she received the key to the city of Ravenna. She instilled the love of learning and reading with weekly library visits, reading to us four every night, and for making books and magazines and newspapers a part of our daily life. She also planted the seeds of possibility, what seems commonplace today but not so much way back when, that a woman could become a lawyer. My dear mother-in-law Beverly Robinson whose last words to me before she passed at the age of 92 were, "When are you going to finish your book?"

Caroline and Kendall, my darling daughters, you inspire me and teach me something new every day. It's been such an honor and a delight to be your mom. To our Aussie Beau for always making sure I take my nap. And to Chris, my rock, who never let me forget my dream. Truly this book would not exist without your love and support. *I'm so lucky* to have you in my life.

Jacquelyn Cynkar Photography

LISA SLAGE ROBINSON writes to explore invisible landscapes and magical feminism. Her work has appeared in *Iron Horse Literary Review, Atticus Review, Smokelong Quarterly, The Adroit Journal, PRISM International, Necessary Fiction*, and elsewhere. A former corporate attorney and litigator, Lisa practiced law in the States and Canada. Currently, she serves as a director for Autumn House Press. She lives in Pittsburgh with her husband and keeps the lights on for their daughters who still like to come home.